# BILL BROOKS

## LAW FOR HIRE:
## SAVING MASTERSON

**HarperTorch**
*An Imprint of HarperCollinsPublishers*

This is a work of fiction. Names, characters, places, and incidents are products of the author's imagination or are used fictitiously and are not to be construed as real. Any resemblance to actual events, locales, organizations, or persons, living or dead, is entirely coincidental.

HARPERTORCH
*An Imprint of* HarperCollins*Publishers*
10 East 53rd Street
New York, New York 10022-5299

Copyright © 2004 by Bill Brooks
ISBN 0-06-054178-4

First HarperTorch paperback printing: March 2004

HarperCollins®, HarperTorch™, and ❦™ are trademarks of Harper-Collins Publishers Inc.

Printed in the United States of America

Visit HarperTorch on the World Wide Web at www.harpercollins.com

10  9  8  7  6  5  4  3  2  1

# "WORD IS YOU KILLED A LAWMAN FROM NEW MEXICO," BONE BUTCHER SAID.

"Who paid you to kill him?"

"Nobody."

"You killed him for free? Then I ought to get a discount on them Mastersons."

"I might kill you for free if you don't stick to the deal we had," Two Bits said. "Hell, I might kill everybody in this dang town. It ain't the friendliest place I ever been."

"We still got us a deal." Bone Butcher could see the impatience in the little man's eyes. "Thing is, I need another feller killed on top of the three I already mentioned. A lanky cuss name of Teddy Blue."

"It don't make no difference to me how many you want killed. Where will I find this yahoo?"

"I asked around. He's staying at the Dodge House, room seven, top of the stairs."

"Seven sounds like an unlucky number. Least it will be when I finish with him."

"Was me, I'd start by killing the easy ones first."

"I don't need you to tell me my job," Two Bits said. "They'll all be dead by morning."

*Also by Bill Brooks*

LAW FOR HIRE: DEFENDING CODY
LAW FOR HIRE: PROTECTING HICKOK

*For Kattlynn, Kennedy, Ian, and Mackenzie*

# LAW FOR HIRE:
## SAVING MASTERSON

# Prologue

———◦•◦———

**B**at was suffering a storm that hadn't yet hit the prairies when Dog Kelly found him drinking his morning coffee.

"That damn Dirty Dave Rudabaugh and some others robbed the morning flier twenty miles outside of town."

"You tell my brother Ed about this?" Bat said.

"Not yet, I figured he was with you."

The bulldog pistol Bat liked to carry was lying on the table next to his coffee, there between his cup and the sugar bowl: pearl grips, nickel-plated, .38 Smith and Wesson, single-action. He liked its weight and feel and he liked looking at it when he wasn't wearing it under his waistcoat. He liked its lethal beauty, thought it poetic.

"Shit, I hate to have to chase outlaws in a storm," Bat muttered.

"Storm? Hell they ain't no storm, it's all sunshine and pretty outside," Dog said.

"It won't be for long."

It was Bat's hip that told him about storms yet to arrive. Sweetwater, Texas, two years previous was where he learned to be a storm prognosticator. He rubbed the hip now, trying to rub some of the ache out of it as he stood, took up the pistol and slipped it into his coat pocket.

"I'll go find Ed and we'll get after 'em."

Dog Kelly followed alongside, explaining what the engineer had told him about which direction the gang was headed after they robbed the train. "South," he said, "toward Liberal would be my guess."

"They ain't going to Liberal," Bat said, crossing the street to the barbershop.

"Why ain't they?"

"They're headed for the pistol barrel of Oklahoma—no man's land. They think if they can reach there, they'll be safe, no law can touch 'em. Even the federal marshals are a bit shy about going into that country."

"You think you and Ed can get 'em before they make it that far?"

"Well, if we can't, they'll most likely get themselves an early grave down in that country. Dirty Dave and anyone who'd run with him isn't the same breed who habituates that territory. The true outlaws will pick those boys' bones clean."

Dog Kelly admired Bat for his use of two-bit words, like *habituate*. Bat was the sort of feller Dodge and Kansas in general needed more of. Educated, refined gentlemen who could also shoot the balls off a gnat.

"Habituate," Dog said, tasting the word like it was hard candy.

Ed was getting a shave and reading an old edition of *Harper's Weekly* when Bat and Dog came into the barbershop.

"Finish up, we got to go buy some oilskins before we go after Dirty Dave and his bunch," Bat said.

Ed looked at him over the top of the magazine. Then he looked at Dog. Then he looked through the big plate-glass window at the clear blue sky and the sunshine that lay over all of Dodge.

"Why we going after Dirty Dave, and why the hell we need oilskins on such a pretty day?"

"Rudabaugh and his minions robbed the Katy out west of here, and it's gone come a bad storm before we catch 'em."

*Minions*, Dog repeated to himself.

"Goddamn, where'd they'd come up with such an idea? Dave don't have the brains to pour piss out of a boot with the directions written on the heel, and I doubt anyone dumb enough to run with him would either."

"They probably read about train robbing in *Harper's*," Bat said. "You know *Harper's* is always running stories on outlaws like Jesse James."

"I wouldn't think Dave was educated enough to read."

"We're wasting time."

Ed wiped the soap off his face and grabbed his

coat, and he and Bat walked down to the stables where they kept saddle horses and told the kid working there to saddle them up and have them ready to go in ten minutes. Then they walked over to the mercantile and bought two boxes of cartridges—one box for each of their pistols and rifles—and a pair of oilskins on a line of credit Ed kept as city marshal.

Dog Kelly asked if they wanted him to round up a posse.

"No," Bat said. "It's just Dave Rudabaugh and some old boys of his. I doubt they'd throw up a fight if cornered. Ed and me can handle 'em."

"You sure we'll need these oilskins?" Ed asked.

"I'm taking mine, you do what you want."

The kid had their mounts ready and they headed on out, riding cross-country to save time and try and cut off the outlaws before they reached the state line.

They rode hard most of the morning, pushing the horses as much as they could, figuring Dirty Dave and his bunch probably wouldn't be expecting a pursuit so early in the game. Outlaws by nature were generally lackadaisical types and not great thinkers.

The way his hip was aching, Bat figured that they were riding right into the front of the coming storm, for it felt like the storm's teeth was gnawing on his bones. An hour later the first drops of cold rain *thunked* their hats.

The prairies had turned bleak under the now

smudged autumn sky. Brown grass that had once stood tall as a man's chest was swept by a hard west wind, and they could see a streaky curtain of rain in the distance, that Bat judged to be at least five miles wide.

They rode another half hour before they saw the Dutchman's soddy. Emil Schirtz kept a consumptive wife and five or six kids who had turned him from being a part-time Lutheran preacher into a full-time alcoholic and trapper—wolf pelts mostly.

"You think we should stop at the Dutchman's and take shelter until the storm blows over?" Ed asked.

"I'd sure hate to be cooped up with that sick wife and squalling kids of his, wouldn't you?" Bat said. Bat was by nature a fastidious man who preferred a clean bed with fresh sheets to sleep in.

"We'd have to sleep on his dirt floor and probably end up with scorpions in our hair."

Ed looked up at the sky. It was near black off to the west and north even though the rain that had thunked their hats had temporarily abated. It felt like some monster overhead just waiting to draw down on them.

Ed said, "It could come a cyclone like that one we saw that time we were buffalo hunting. You remember that?"

"How could I forget?"

"Come along and killed Tully and his boys, swept 'em clean up and blew 'em a mile—even their wagon full of hides."

"Hell yes, I remember, but this don't look like any cyclone could come of it."

They weighed their decision as they rode their horses at a walk because earlier they'd run them pretty hard. Then suddenly they were pelted by hail the size of marbles.

"I'd rather sleep on a dirt floor with a roof over my head than get thumped by hail balls," Ed said, remembering a storm he'd gotten caught in the previous spring, when hail the size of tomatoes fell from the sky. The hail had battered him pretty good and his body was a palette of bruises for a week.

"I reckon we could stop in at the Dutchman's and see how the storm tracks," Bat said.

"I don't know of any other place out this way we could take shelter in, do you?"

Bat shook his head. His thoughts had been on other lives lived than the one he was living currently. He'd been reading articles in the local papers about the successes of Buffalo Bill and Pawnee Bill and others who were performing with their Wild West Combinations back East. *I was made for a life more gentrified than riding after train robbers in a storm*, he told himself. He'd long held the hankering to go East, to go live among a more civilized breed of men and see how his cork would float in such waters. But instead, he'd landed here in Dodge with his brothers Ed and Jim.

Still, he told himself, he should be grateful to

have attained his current station in life at such a young age: sheriff of Ford County—not bad for only being twenty-two years old. But still it wasn't the life he wanted. The bullet that had shattered his hip was more than a gentle reminder that his current profession generally didn't carry a man to old age, or any real accomplishments. He had within him a yearning to travel to distant places and not simply across windswept prairies. He thought maybe he'd like to try his hand at writing.

"Listen," Ed said.

They heard the first rumble of thunder, saw lightning snake through the clouds like tin flashing in the sun. It felt ominous; they both knew what lightning could do if it struck a feller.

They spurred their horses toward the Dutchman's.

The wind picked up considerable by the time they crossed the quarter mile of prairie to where the soddy stood. The soddy looked crumbly under a roof of grass. It was a house essentially cut from the earth, and to the earth it was bound to return. It stood lonely and forlorn, as though lost.

There were several scrawny chickens pecking the ground around the building. There was an old single-blade plow lying over on its side in a patch of thistles, its blade rusting. There was a pile of empty tin cans stacked by the west wall, and just beyond was an outhouse with the door missing. The wind shifted and blew the outhouse stink their direction, causing them to wrinkle their noses. Hail tapped their hats and danced along the ground. There was an old plug horse standing in a poorly constructed corral, its head drooping. The nag, like everything else, looked like it was just waiting for a good excuse to fall over. Between house and corral was a buckboard with one of its wheels missing.

"I don't know how a body can live like this," Bat said.

"I don't neither."

"Hello this house!"

Bat and Ed both knew you just didn't walk up and knock on a fellow's door—not out in these parts you didn't. Such incaution could get you shot.

They sat their horses, waiting for someone to open the door.

The thunder grew louder, the skies darker. The bellies of the clouds came in lower now over the prairies and moving fast. The hail started and stopped and started again.

"Hello the house!" Bat said a second time, louder.

Still nobody came to the door.

"Maybe they're asleep," Ed suggested.

"This time of day?"

Ed wanted to suggest that maybe the Schirtzes had packed up and moved, but the presence of the wagon, the chickens and that old horse told him otherwise.

Bat said, "Keep that shotgun of yours trained

on things," then dismounted and went to the door and, standing off to one side, knocked hard. It wasn't much of a door, but it had a fancy porcelain knob you'd thought was right out of a St. Louis catalogue.

"Hey inside!"

Nothing.

Bat looked at Ed and Ed at him.

Then the wind shifted again and they both could smell an unmistakable stench leaking from inside the house. Ed dismounted, shotgun still in hand, and Bat drew his revolver and said, "You want to go around back and check things out?" and Ed nodded and slipped around to the back.

"I'm ready when you are," Ed called above the increasing wind.

Bat's hip ached bad as a rotted tooth, but what he figured was inside that house waiting to be discovered troubled him more.

Bat tried the doorknob, twisted it and the door just fell open and the stench came out like bad breath.

"You see anything back there?" he yelled to Ed.

"Nothing."

"I'm going in, don't shoot me with that scattergun."

It was dark inside, just a thin shaft of light falling in through a window covered with an oilcloth. The smell alone would have knocked out a horse.

Then Bat saw them as his eyes adjusted to the

light. He started counting until he counted all eight of them, the last being the Dutchman—a big old boy sitting in a chair, slumped over, his head resting on the table, his arms down to his sides, a pistol still hooked by one crooked finger.

Bat stepped back outside and sucked in all the prairie air he could get and fought back the sickness that'd risen bitterly in his throat. It was raining now, cold and heavy.

Ed came around because there wasn't any back door or any windows to see in and he saw Bat standing there bent over, his hands on his knees, his color the same as the ashen sky.

"What is it?" Ed said.

"Everybody's gone in there," Bat said.

"Every one of 'em?"

The rain changed over to hail again and struck the earth and everything on it.

"Every one of 'em," Bat said. "I guess the Dutchman just couldn't take it anymore."

"You sure it was him and not some other— Dirty Dave and his gang, maybe?"

Bat nodded. "It was him, he's still holding his piece."

"That son of a bitch."

"It's forty miles back to Dodge," Bat said. The hail became an icy rain and they could feel it was going to get a lot worse before it got better and cleared off the prairies. Thunder shook the ground.

They led their horses over to the corral and turned them out and then hurried back to the cabin; the icy rain had begun to collect. There wasn't any way they were going to ride all the way back to Dodge in an ice storm.

They both stood just inside the doorjamb, neither of them wanting to go completely inside the soddy with the dead. They took off their bandannas and tied them around their noses and kept their faces toward the open air even as sleet crackled along the ground.

"Jesus," Ed said. "I can't believe none of this."

Neither of them wanted to look at the dead.

"How long you reckon they been this way?"

"A week maybe, judging by the odor."

"Them little kids . . ." Ed said.

The storm kept up for an hour then began to slacken some and it was about all either of them could take, so that when the hiatus came, they walked from the soddy to the corral and forked their mounts, Ed saying, "We best just head on back to Dodge and send out some men to bury 'em and forget about that goddamn Dirty Dave Rudabaugh for the time being, don't you think?"

Bat didn't put up an argument.


Dog Kelly found Bat and Ed drinking in the Lone Star, the frozen rain dripping off their oilskins into puddles at their feet. Dog's hat was covered in ice. His ears stuck out red as beets. Bad weather meant bad business, and bad business meant empty pockets. As both mayor of Dodge and owner of one of its more respected saloons—the Alhambra—Dog was unhappy.

"I hear you boys found a house full of death out on them prairies," Dog said.

"In spades," Ed said.

"And no sign of Dirty Dave or his crew?"

"You think we should have just kept going after 'em, after finding the Dutchman?" Bat said.

"No, I guess you boys did the right thing."

"You damn right we did."

"Let me buy you boys a round."

Ed said, "You'd be buying Bat his own liquor."

"Oh, I guess you're right, since him and Jimmy own the place."

"We sent some men out to bury 'em," Ed said. "J. R. Reed and some other boys."

"That's good," Dog Kelly said. "I'll arrange for proper services for 'em with the reverend."

Dog knocked some of the ice from his hat, watched it fall to the floor.

"I need to go make my night rounds," Ed said. "I hope I don't dream about 'em tonight."

Dog drank a beer while Bat worked on a bottle of whiskey he'd been keeping close at hand ever since he and Ed had ridden back into town and put the word out about the Dutchman and his family.

Bat was quiet by nature, but even more so given the circumstances.

"Bad things happen out here on these prairies," Dog said. "The damn wind makes 'em go nuts half the time. Wind and loneliness and hard weather and too little money and too many mouths to feed. They come out here thinking of the free land they're getting. They forget that they ain't nothing free when it comes down to it. I think Schirtz was from Ohio. What was his wife's name . . . ?"

"Molly," Bat said. It wasn't a name he would easily forget, for a simple reason: Molly had been the name of a girl back in Sweetwater, Texas, shot dead two years earlier when Bat got educated about weather prognostication by the same gun.

"Molly seems like a nice name," Dog said. "I didn't know any of them kids' names, did you?"

"One of 'em was a boy named Lester I think," Bat said. "That's about all I remember of 'em."

With the ice storm and news of the deaths, the Lone Star, like all the other drinking dens, was quiet at that particular hour. It was just Bat and Dog Kelly standing at the bar. Jim Masterson was mopping the floor on the other side of the room in anticipation that more customers would arrive eventually.

"I got some other bad news," Dog said.

Bat looked at him with sorrowful dark eyes.

"I ain't got no hard proof," Dog said, "but word is around that they's some in this town don't want honest law to rule things no more."

"Earp didn't have any trouble cleaning up the

bad element," Bat said, pouring himself another tumbler of whiskey. "What makes you think Ed and me will?"

"I've ever confidence in you boys," Dog said. "Thing is, I don't know who-all's behind this thing, and that can be a mighty dangerous situation for you boys."

"Well, I guess we can put our own word out that we're ready for 'em, whoever they are," Bat said, feeling more surly now because he didn't care for such talk on top of what he'd seen earlier at the Dutchman's.

"I'm damn sick and tired of the talk of killing," Bat said somberly. "If there's any more of it to be done, it will be me and Ed doing it. You put that word out, Dog. Put it out loud and clear, you hear me?"

"Yes sir. But I just want you to know, I ain't putting all my eggs in the same basket. I've sent a wire to the Pinkertons."

"What the hell for?"

"As mayor of Dodge, I have a responsibility," Dog said. "You and Ed will continue doing the law round here, but if I can get a man on the inside and find out who they are, we can bust 'em out before they go to assassinating anybody."

"Fuck 'em," Bat said. "Let 'em assassinate if they think they're up to it."

Dog saw the way Bat Masterson's eyes grew darker still—like a storm.

"You boys is good boys," Dog said. "Go along

with me on this, Bat. How's it going to hurt for me to find out who our enemies are and rid the town of 'em?"

Bat stared into the whiskey, a mirror of his own chagrin.

"You do what you want to," he said. "And me and Ed will do what we have to."

"It's for the best," Dog Kelly said. "For everyone concerned. We come too far to let this town slip back into the clutches of the bad element."

Bat listened to the ice storm, the way it sounded against the windows, and thought of the dead back at the Dutchman's and knew he'd go ahead and get drunk because that's all you could do sometimes.

"I'll let you boys know when the Pinkerton arrives. I owe you that much and I want your cooperation on this thing, Bat."

Bat shifted his gaze from the whiskey to Dog Kelly.

"I'd just as soon do no more talking this day," Bat said.

And Dog knew that a silent man was much more dangerous than one who talked, and thus allowed Bat his solitude by once more braving the ice storm and feeling its sting on his skin like needles, wondering half to himself why he'd come to such a killing place as Kansas.

# Chapter 1

———— •◦• ————

They had been almost a year down in that country.

John Sears had wanted to cross the Rio Grande into old Mexico as soon as Teddy Blue busted him out of the jail in Las Vegas.

"Even Hoodoo Brown wouldn't have the cajones to come looking for us down there," John had said. But Teddy had made a commitment to his boss, George Bangs, the director of Pinkerton's Detective Agency, in agreeing to go meet with Colonel Cody, and so that's what they did. And once that matter had been taken care of, Teddy rode with John down across the border and found the little village of Refugio, where they were presently.

The first of the letters that arrived was written in pencil on butcher's paper.

*Ma's dead. She wanted you to know. She died right after you were here. Married Antrim, then died. I guess he didn't do her no good like she thought. She said your name in her last hour. I guess that's about all I have to say. She wanted you to know so I promised her I'd write and tell you. Hope you get this. Antrim cries big tears. So what?*

*Wm. H. Bonney.*

The letter had a dollar's worth of postage and was mailed originally to Teddy's address in Chicago. His mother had forwarded it with the others and included a note of her own praying that he was well.

John was tossing a stick so the little dog would chase it and bring it to him. They'd been sitting in the shade of an adobe when the letters arrived. Old man named Ortega rode a mule to deliver the mail every day like clockwork if there was any. Most days there wasn't any. They'd been down in Juarez since before Christmas, had taken their pay from Cody's hunting trip to sustain them an easy life. Had crossed the Rio Grande without getting their feet wet and kept riding. Refugio seemed the right sort of place for men like them who didn't want to be found.

"What is it, old son?" John said when he caught the look on his young partner's face after having read the letter.

Teddy held the letter a second, then let the wind take it. He and John watched it fly like a drunken butterfly until it snagged on the upper branches of a mimosa tree.

"You want some of this tequila?" John said, nodding toward an olla by his feet.

Teddy reached out for the jar and John handed it to him then took a sip himself when Teddy handed it back.

They'd raised beards and let their hair grow long and wore serapes and couldn't hardly be told from the natives, with their sun-browned faces and how they spoke the local lingo.

"Bad news?" John said.

"About as bad as it gets."

John passed him back the olla then rolled himself a shuck and smoked it.

"You want to talk about it?"

"It's the woman I went to see in Silver City," Teddy said. "Kathleen Bonney."

"Lung fever as I recall. She die?"

"Yes."

"I'm sorry as hell to hear of it."

The little dog worried John with the retrieved stick until John worked it loose from the hound's jaws and flung it again. He liked watching smart dogs just like he enjoyed watching a good horse or a beautiful woman or clean white clouds in a glass blue sky.

John looked at the other letters Teddy hadn't yet opened, weighted by a rock. He didn't say anything. The sky was hot-metal white that time of day—the siesta hour. The air buzzed with flies. A community well stood just up the street from where the two men sat. They'd spent the last hour sitting in the shade and watching the comings and goings of the locals to that well: women mostly, drawing up buckets of water and filling clay jugs.

"I've been thinking of going north again," Teddy said.

"Because of her?"

"It's too late for me to do anything for her. I was thinking about going north before today."

"Where north?"

A boy came down the dusty street leading a burro loaded down with ocotillo sticks. The boy looked at them, at the olla they passed between them, his face dark as saddle leather, hair black as crow feathers. His name was Chico something and he worked for the priest doing odd jobs. Some said he was really the priest's own child, that the mother had died during birth—God's retribution for the padre's sins. Who was to say what was true, what wasn't?

John said, "That kid reminds me of me when I was his age—dirt poor and aimless."

"You made any plans yet?" Teddy asked.

"Me? Just to stay alive and out of jail, I reckon is all."

"You think you'll ever get over it, what happened in Las Vegas?"

John thought about the shooting, the way he'd come home to find his woman with the other man. John told himself a thousand times if he hadn't been drinking he wouldn't have pulled his pistol and let blind anger wash away all his reason and the woman would not be dead. He never meant for it to come out bad. The worst part was the man had lived. The man became a witness against him in the trial. He still remembered how that fellow smirked a little when he told his side of the story.

"No," John said. "I never will get over something like that, I don't reckon."

The days had been as lazy as the Rio Grande itself. They'd subsisted on frijoles and fry bread, a little pork now and then, sometimes wild turkeys they'd shoot out in the chaparral. They drank tiswin and tequila at a local cantina run by an ex-Confederate soldier who kept a shot-through flag of the Stars and Bars tacked up on the wall behind the back bar. The man claimed he could never find any peace back in the States, the way things had turned out with the war.

"I'd rather die down here than be buried in ground the Yankees stole from my folks," the Confederate said. His name was St. John and there was some rumor he was the actor Wilkes Booth, who'd shot President Lincoln, but neither Teddy nor John believed such a story and none of the locals much cared who he was.

Once in a while the Federales came through and stopped long enough to drink and fornicate with some of the local girls. John and Teddy kept a low profile when they were in the area.

The priest was also a gringo, who brought as much God as he could to the village, and was considered pretty much the *jefe* when it came to disputes that required judgment decreed. He sometimes came down and drank with them. His name was Seamus McGrady and he kept a local girl for companionship, which further fueled rumors that the orphan kid was his. The villagers simply called him "Padre." The priest was older than either of them and had lived for a time in Texas, which made John feel a kinship with him, for John was a Texan by birth.

One afternoon just after Christmas John had gone to the church and told the priest: "I ain't Catholic . . . hell, I ain't nothing when it comes down to it, but I'd like to confess something anyway." The priest blessed him and said he didn't think it would matter much to God that John wasn't Catholic and to go ahead and make his confession. So John did and the priest said that God forgave the sinner who was truly repentant for his sins and John felt some better about it afterward.

The priest came down now to where they sat in the shade and drank and watched the locals going to the well and doing their trading there in the plaza.

John passed the priest the olla of tequila and he took a drink and handed it back.

"Teddy's thinking of leaving," John said to the priest. "Going north again."

"That's something I've thought about several times myself," the priest said.

"Why haven't you, then?" Teddy asked.

"I don't know, except I guess I've fallen in love with Selena," the priest said, meaning the girl he kept companionship with. "If I left and went north again, I couldn't take her with me and remain a priest."

"It's an easy life down here," Teddy said. "Too easy to suit me."

They drank a little more, then the priest said he had to go and prepare afternoon mass and they watched him go.

John said, "You going to open them other letters?"

Teddy looked at them, then picked one he could see was from Anne Morgan, postmarked New York City and already a month old. He opened it.

*Dearest Teddy,*

*I've thought about you nearly every day and wondered how you are. I hope this letter finds you in good health, that your shoulder has healed and that your life is more pleasant now than when we last saw each other. I'm still not completely over the shock of Edgar's death, or the guilt I've carried because I did not love him, and because of what transpired between you and I. New York is gray and dreary, and to be honest, I wish you were here with me now so that we could talk. I wonder where you are at the very moment you'll read this. I trust that your mother was*

*good enough to forward my letter on to you.
I do wish you'd write me and let me know
how you are. I've made no decisions yet on
what I should do next, but I pray that the an-
swers will come, and I hope that whatever
my future is, that you are somehow a part of
it. With the greatest affection,*

*Anne.*

He'd thought of her often since their encounters
on the hunting expedition with Cody. He never
meant to fall in love with a married woman. Hell,
he never meant to fall in love at all, but he had,
twice already, and neither time had it come out
good.

He folded the letter carefully and put it into his
shirt pocket, then opened the last letter—this
from George Bangs.

"What's it say?" John asked after Teddy finished reading.

"George wants me to go to Dodge City. There's
a mayor there that wants some help breaking a
conspiracy ring bent on killing the local law."

"Shit," John said. "What's this frontier coming
to, the law can't handle their own problems?"

"I don't know," Teddy said. "You up to coming
along?"

"Not me. I'm still wanted for a hanging, remember."

"Maybe I can fix that somehow."

"Well, you figure out how, let me know. I'd like us to stay saddle pards, but under the circumstance, I hope you understand why I can't hardly go north again with you."

They sat and drank some more and smoked cigarettes, and that night they went and watched the dance in the plaza and felt the music vibrating in their blood. They saw the pretty faces of the senoritas, their teeth so white in their sweet brown faces as they danced with their suitors they could make a man's heart break just watching them. The music seemed to sprout wings and take flight against the canopy of nightfall.

The priest came with his young companion and joined them and said, "The music makes everything better. Everyone forgets their burdens on such nights as this—even if for only a little while."

The priest looked at his young woman, who was among the prettiest there. She was a mute and her silence somehow made her seem more beautiful, and she was somehow beautiful to them all.

She tugged at the priest's arm to dance with her and he did, and John and Teddy watched with a certain envy as the two of them swirled around the plaza under the sky with its stars and music.

They knew it might be a long time before they shared such a moment and they wanted it to stay with them long after this night.

It struck Teddy what a long way he and John had come from the days they first met each other on the cattle trails and John had taught him about everything of value there was to know for a young greenhorn Easterner who thought he wanted to be a cowboy. Teddy would never and could never forget the debt he felt he owed John and hoped that, with busting him out of that Las Vegas jail and a certain hanging, he'd paid some of the debt in kind, though he knew John never saw it as Teddy owing him anything. It seemed too, that Teddy had lived an entire lifetime in the past three years since his brother Horace had been shot and killed and he first headed west.

Horace's murder and law school and Chicago where he'd grown up seemed like another world away, another lifetime. And even the fact that he was officially a Pinkerton detective still, and had worked on cases to protect two of the West's most legendary characters, seemed like the life lived by someone other than himself.

John said, "Look."

And they saw how happy the priest's young woman was.

And they heard the music enter their blood.

# Chapter 2

Teddy and John shook hands and John said, "You be careful across that border—them Texas Rangers might mistake you for some sort of bandito and shoot you clean out of the saddle."

"I look that rough, eh?"

"Rough enough."

"Maybe I should shave and buy a silk suit and a bowler."

"Shit," John said. "You went up in that country dressed such, them Rangers might shoot you for being too damn dandified. They're touchy fellers, them Rangers."

"I'll keep an eye out for 'em."

"You do that, old son. You get into a bad fix, you know where to send word. I ain't going nowhere out of here anytime soon."

"One thing," Teddy said, climbing into the saddle.

"I can feel a lecture coming on."

"I know she's pretty, John. But she's his woman."

"I know it," John said. "I know she's his woman. It's something I respect and I won't go 'round her. 'Sides, I've got a terrible history with women, even if she wasn't his woman. Of course if he was to take it in his mind to up and go north again and leave her behind, I ain't promising I'd just let her be sad."

Teddy saw the mute girl who lived with the priest standing in the doorway of their adobe watching him and John in the glare of the morning. The priest was giving a mass and Teddy knew what temptation a woman could be for a man down in that country, where there wasn't any law but one man's respect for another.

Teddy touched spurs to his mount and didn't look back, and John stood there watching him until he had ridden out of sight.

Two days riding brought him to the Rio Grande and he crossed it and felt almost immediately the change in him when he rode out of the river and onto Texas soil. He wasn't sure if the feeling he had was a good one or bad.

He rode all the way to El Paso and sold the horse and bought a train ticket after he wired George Bangs he was headed for Dodge and that he'd be a day in El Paso if George had any further instructions for him.

He walked around the sun-soaked plazas and El Paso didn't seem that much different than the village he'd left in some respects, except El Paso was much larger and had an energy to it that the village did not have.

There were plenty of saloons and billiard parlors, hardware stores and other places of commerce—hotels included. He rented a room and then went and found a barbershop and had the barber cut his hair and shave his beard, and from there he found a public bath and soaked while his clothes were being cleaned.

Afterward he found a cantina and ordered a meal: steak and fried potatoes, tortillas, and ice beer. Finishing his meal, he strolled around the town now golden with the light of early evening. He was struck by the beauty of some of the women and realized how long it had been since he'd been with a woman. He felt unfaithful even thinking about it.

He stopped in a saloon for a cocktail, thinking a drink might be the best way to finish off the evening before he went back to his hotel room.

He stood at the bar and listened to the music of a piano being played by a man with garters on his sleeves. The piano music, the *clickity-clack* of the roulette wheel being turned in a corner of the room, and the laughter and talk of patrons were all part of the same cacophony he welcomed after so many months down in the quiet little village, where the only music to be heard was the church bell, and occasionally guitars and trumpets when there was a Saturday night dance.

A tall thin man came in and stood at the bar and ordered a beer. He and the bartender spoke as old friends, the bartender saying, "Pat, when'd you get back into town?"

"Oh, I just got in," the tall man said.

"You still buffalo hunting for a living?"

"No, the buffalo have all been shot out. I'm looking for some regular work, you know of any?"

"Might be a bartending job open over to the El Toro is about all I know of."

"Bartending ain't for me, if I don't have to."

"These is hard times, Pat. Ain't much work to be had unless you're in the killing business."

"I ain't."

"I wish I knew of something else to tell you."

Another man came over and slapped the tall man on the back.

"Garrett," he said to the tall man. "When'd you get into town?"

"Just," the tall man said.

The three of them stood there chatting until the bartender got summoned for another round of drinks at the far end of the bar.

"I think maybe I'll head over to New Mexico," the tall man said to the shorter one. "Might be able to pick up some work. My pockets is so empty they ain't even got lint in 'em."

"That's some hard country over there," the short man said. "Lots of killing going on."

"Killing's common these days."

"More so there. They ain't hardly got no law, the way I hear it. Wasn't you a lawman once't?"

"I did a little before I got into shooting buffalo."

"Might think about wearing a badge again. I kindy reckon they could use some extra laws in that country. You ever hear of Hoodoo Brown?"

It caught Teddy's attention, the mention of that name.

"I heard of him," the tall man said. "What about him?"

"He was the law up in Las Vegas. They say he's a hard man to work for, always needing to hire deputies. Might be you could catch on there if you were looking to wear a badge."

"I don't know," the tall man said. "Politics never was my style."

Teddy studied the tall man, didn't see much that impressed him. He finished his drink and walked out into the still evening, thinking he'd stop on his way back to the hotel to see if there was any word yet arrived from George Bangs.

There was a telegram from George waiting for him.

*Have wired Mayor Kelly you're on your way. Still working on getting you cleared in Las Vegas matter. Have sent operative there to investigate. Inform me of your arrival in Dodge. Possible news on Horace's murder case, may have located sister of shooter. Will inform you soon as I have more information.*

*G. Bangs.*

The sun was laying down the last of its light on El Paso's streets when he emerged from the office. At that hour, the city looked golden and inviting, possibly to some serious trouble if a man wasn't careful. Night had a way of bringing out the loose in a man, and a woman too.

Teddy walked toward his hotel. He was a city block away when he saw the tall man named Pat Garrett emerge from the saloon and start across the street. But as he did, a city policeman, a much shorter man in a dark coat wearing a round-crowned hat with a badge pinned to it stopped Garrett. Teddy was too far away to hear what they were talking about, but suddenly the police-man pulled his revolver and Garrett raised his hands while the policeman disarmed him of what looked to be a seven-inch-barrel Colt Peacemaker.

As Teddy came closer he heard the policeman say, "Vagrancy is what I'm charging you with. Now get your long skinny ass on the move . . ." then watched as the policeman marched Garrett off at the point of his gun.

Teddy felt sorry for a man who simply wanted to find work but only managed to find trouble instead.

The next morning, he boarded the flyer out of El Paso, somewhat glad he was on the move again and maybe staying a step ahead of his own problems.

# Chapter 3

————◆————

Bone Butcher didn't like the Masterson brothers one lick. Not a single one of the three. As part owners in the Lone Star, Jim and Bat were competitors, and Ed being the city marshal and Bat being the county sheriff gave them all an edge on things, the way Bone figured it. In Bone's eyes, the Mastersons and Dog Kelly, mayor and owner of the Alhambra, were thick as thieves, protected one another's interest in the gambling and whoring trades. As long as things were the way they were, Bone could feature himself out of business in Dodge sooner rather than later.

He'd been around this block before, when the Earp brothers were wearing badges in the town. Bone had hired Clay Allison to take care of the Earps. Clay had himself a big reputation as a stone killer down in Texas—but apparently such reputation stopped at the border, because when Clay showed up in Dodge he almost pissed in his boots when Wyatt confronted him and told him to clear town or clear leather.

"I think the son of a bitch Allison was fruity," is

what Bone told his gofer, one Bad Hand Frank Partridge about Clay Allison's rather quick departure out of Dodge.

"Clay Allison is the meanest bastard in Texas," Bad Hand Frank Partridge replied. Bad Hand Frank Partridge had once been an accountant in a Boston law firm before liquor and cocaine pills turned him bad. Now he kept Bone's books and accounts of his various business interests, which included the Silk Garter Saloon, with its gambling and prostitution, and a dope den, the Dream Palace.

"He may be the meanest bastard in Texas, but Dodge ain't hardly Texas, now, is it?" Bone said, still bitter it had cost him a hundred dollars in expense money for Clay Allison to come to Dodge.

"I guess not."

"You hear how he talked? Like a goddamn woman, real high voice. I think he was fruity."

"Maybe so, I wouldn't know nothing about that sort of thing, Bone."

"We'll be dealing faro out the back of a buckboard and selling whores down out of a tent we don't do something soon about Dog Kelly and them Mastersons."

"What you intend to do?"

"I intend to kill 'em," Bone said.

"All of 'em?"

"Ever damn last one of 'em. Hell, what if I was to pay you to kill 'em for me?"

Bad Hand Frank extended his ruined right

hand with just the last two fingers and the thumb attached.

"I ain't shit with a gun since Leavenworth."

Frank had often told the story about his missing fingers, especially when he was drinking hard and maudlin. "Chopped off by a goddamn sumbitch in the pen," he would bemoan on such occasions.

"Why'd he chop 'em off?" Bone had asked, the first time Frank told the story.

"I'll tell you why he chopped 'em off," Frank had said, with a mixture of anger and self pity. Frank prefaced the description of the act of violence that had led to his ruination with a tawdry tale of how men locked up in prison for a long time could get.

"The man who chopped 'em off was a cook and quite clever with a cleaver. He'd been in the pen for twenty years by the time I arrived and wasn't ever getting out. Me and him got celled up together.

"He was always talking about how lonely it was and bringing me extra eats from the kitchen and at first I didn't think nothing about it," Frank had explained in blubbering tones. "Then one night I learned why he was being so nice and I told him to forget about such notions and we got to fighting and he just chopped 'em off before I could bash his skull in on the bars."

"I wish you hadn't told me none of that story," Bone had said afterward. "I never did care for stories of perversion."

Frank stood there now, holding his scarred hand forth with its missing trigger and middle fingers. His hand looked like a claw of sorts.

"You can see I ain't never could make no damn shootist," Frank said.

"You could stab 'em, you wouldn't have to shoot 'em necessarily."

"No, you best hire you a professional killer you want them Mastersons done in."

"It'll take more'n one, my guess is."

"How bad you want 'em dead?"

"Bad."

"I know a feller might do it for a thousand dollars."

"Thousand dollars!"

"He don't come cheap, but his work is guaranteed."

"Guaranteed, huh? I like the sound of that. How you know this feller?"

"I was in the pen with him for a time."

"What was he in for?"

"Killing folks."

"They let him out for killing folks? He couldn't have killed nobody too bad, they let him out."

"They didn't let him out, he escaped."

"Why didn't you mention him back when I was looking for somebody to shoot them Earps and hired that damn fruit Allison instead?"

"You never asked me," Bad Hand Frank said. "If you'd asked me then, I'd told you about this feller."

"How you gonna find him if he's escaped from the pen? He's probably long in the wind by now."

"He's in Montana fixing to kill some people."

"How you know this?"

"My sister told me."

"How's she know?"

"She's married to him."

"He escaped the pen then went and married your sister?"

"No, he was married to her before he went to the pen."

"Why didn't you say this before?"

"You never asked me."

"Jeez Christ, I got to ask you everything ahead of time?"

"Pretty much. I ain't never been no mind reader."

Bad Hand Frank Partridge was feeling pain where his fingers used to be. He looked at his hand and the fingers that were left were trembling like they were lonely and searching around for the missing ones.

"I need to take me some cocaine pills and drink some more whiskey, because what I already took ain't doing the job," Frank said. "It gets worse all the time, the pain does."

"Thousand dollars," Bone said working the figure around in his mouth as though he were trying to chew it enough to get it swallowed. "That's a lot of money."

"Tell you one thing," Frank said. "When Two

Bits shoots 'em, even Jesus can't raise 'em up again."

"Two Bits, huh? How'd he come by that name?"

"Two Bits Cline. Says he killed his first man for two bits. Says it just sorta stuck, the nickname."

"That sounds like a fruit's name to me."

Frank nodded as he poured himself a glass of Bone's best whiskey to wash down the handful of cocaine pills he shook from a small tin he'd picked from his pocket.

"Two Bits is the only man I ever met who ain't afraid of nothing, not even my sister."

"Still sounds like a fruit's name."

"Him and my sister has got three kids. I don't reckon he's no fruit, and he'd probably shoot you in the head if you was to call him one. He's sort of an ill-tempered feller."

"Go on and get hold of him."

"I can't hardly think, my hand hurts so bad."

"Maybe you ought to go pay the Rose a visit."

"What for? She ain't no doctor."

"No, but she has her ways of taking a man's mind off his troubles."

The Rose of Cimarron was Bone's woman—a former whore who he'd fallen in love with. Bone was always testing her loyalty to him just as he was Bad Hand Frank's loyalty. Frank knew better than to try and show any interest whatsoever in the Rose.

"Ah, I know she's your gal," Frank said. "You can't trick me."

Bone Butcher smiled in a way that both his thin moustaches lifted.

"You ain't fruity are you, Frank?"

"Hell no, but I ain't crazy enough to dally with the Rose, either."

"That's right, because you know I'd chop off some other parts of you if you did, and it wouldn't be no damn fingers either."

Frank felt the first haze of the whiskey and the pills working in combination to bring him relief. Felt the warmth of his blood traveling down to where his missing fingers used to be and wondered whatever happened to that happy kid that used to spend his days fishing in a creek in Ohio and gigging frogs, and all those wonderful days when he had all his fingers still and didn't live in the back room of Bone Butcher's saloon with just a cot and a piss pot.

He liked life a lot better before he became known as Bad Hand Frank, and sometimes he could almost taste the buttermilk his mother churned and see his big daddy stalking the pastures in search of his cows.

*Those were the best times,* he thought.

Then Bone farted and the whole room stunk.

# Chapter 4

Dodge rose out of the plains suddenly. Teddy watched the landscape for a hundred miles without seeing much more than a few soddys scattered here and there amid oceans of dead winter grass. Occasionally he would spot a small herd of grazing antelope, their tails switching. If he thought about it hard enough, he could imagine these selfsame prairies dark with the great herds of buffalo that Cody had spoke so poignantly of when he got likkered up. But Cody and others like him had cleared the grass of the wooly beasts until it was rare to see a single one.

"Jesus, I don't know why we did it," he remembered Cody saying. "We shot ourselves clean out of work and clean out of something we'll be lucky to ever see again."

Teddy had also watched for several hundred miles the train trying to outrun its shadow. Then suddenly there rose Dodge in the distance, and the train never did outrun its shadow.

At last the train screeched to a halt and he stepped from the car into a stiff wind that whistled along the eaves of the train station and tugged at the cuffs of his trousers. Dog Kelly was there to meet him. Little feller standing under a stovepipe hat and wearing a swallowtail coat, his checked trousers stuffed down inside the tops of his boots. Eyes narrow set, sharp nose, clean cheeks. Goat chin whiskers.

"You him? The Pinkerton?" Dog said.

"Teddy Blue," Teddy said, extending a hand.

"Dog Kelly, mayor."

Teddy held onto his hat.

"Windy, I know," Dog said. "Let's go over to my office and I'll buy you something to cut the dry out of your throat."

Dodge was like a lot of other frontier towns with its wide streets and false-fronted buildings. There didn't seem to be anything out of the ordinary to Dodge in Teddy's view, nothing that would distinguish Dodge from any of the other cow towns he'd been to except for the talk he'd heard about it: the tales about it being one of the toughest towns in the West—a "bibulous Babylon." *You wouldn't know it looking at it*, he thought. He half expected to see dead men lying on the sidewalks and whores hanging out every window.

He followed Dog Kelly down to the Alhambra, which lay, as Dog explained it, "south of the deadline," meaning south of the railroad tracks that divided the town in two.

"This your office?"

"Being mayor ain't exactly a high position with a lot of pay to it," Dog said and went behind the bar and drew them each a beer whose head he swiped off with a paddle.

"Let's sit over at my table," Dog said and led Teddy to a back corner.

Dog shucked off his coat and hat. He had small hands, rings on several of his fingers, Teddy noticed. Small and smooth like a gambler's. Frayed cuffs, and his paper collar was yellowing. Teddy saw too, when Dog shucked his coat, a bulge in the pocket of his waistcoat. Guessed it to probably be a derringer, a knuckle duster, perhaps.

"Good trip out?" Dog said.

"Uneventful."

"You don't talk like no frontiersman."

"Does that make a difference to you?"

"No sir, it don't at all. Fact is, I admire a man with a good education. A smart man thinks before he acts, and that's exactly the sort of man I need currently. But I need one willing to act once he's thought through what needs doing."

"You want to tell me why you need a Pinkerton?"

Dog sipped some of his beer and fingered his chin whiskers, touched them like he'd just discovered they were there.

"I want to keep this about who you are and what you're doing here a private matter," he said, looking about. "Ain't nobody knows about you except me and the Mastersons. It's got to stay that-a-way too. Word gets out on you, you're no good to me. We clear on that?"

"This isn't my first day on the job, Mr. Kelly. Lay it out for me what the problem is."

So Dog told him about the *rumors*, about his personal suspicion that the rumors were true—that there was an element in town set on assassinating the Mastersons.

"Meaning . . ." Dog said, "They'll probably hire out to get it done."

"Why not just do it themselves?" Teddy said.

"They ain't of that ilk, I'm guessing. Dog enjoyed using a fancy word like *ilk* ever since he'd heard Bat use it once. "If they tried and failed, they'd either wind up dead or arrested. Knowing the Mastersons, it'd probably be the former. Either way, it would defeat their purpose. They hire an out-of-town gun to do it, they'll keep clean hands in the eyes of the law unless it can be proved otherwise."

"You got a name of the conspirators?"

*Conspirators.* Dog made a mental note of the word. He liked it.

"Nothing solid. It's all just rumors floating about. I'm working on it. But now that you're here, maybe you can find out a lot better."

"Any ideas where I should start to ingratiate myself?"

Dog smiled. This feller had as many fancy words in him as did Bat.

"Anyplace south of these tracks. There's three

or four in particular that run establishments that wouldn't be unhappy to attend the funeral of the Mastersons. Angus Bush, who runs the Black Cat; Frenchy LeBreck, who operates the Paris Club; and Bone Butcher, who owns both the Silk Garter and the Dream Palace, a dope den. They'd be the most likely candidates. You could start with them."

"I'll need to get a room and meet the Mastersons."

"Try the Dodge House up the street, tell 'em I sent you. Meeting Bat and Ed might take a day or three—they're out chasing down some low types."

"I need to report into my boss as well," Teddy said.

"Telegraph's just down the way. Everything you need, Dodge has got. And if we ain't got it yet, either you don't need it or we will have it soon."

"Including assassins?"

"Hope is, you'll make sure that's one thing we won't have long if we got 'em. Like lice, not something you want."

Teddy stood and picked up his valise.

"Just so you know," Dog said. "Bat and them ain't real happy about me sending for help from the Pinkertons."

"Well, when you see him, tell him there's lots of other places I'd just soon be myself."

"You're kindy young for this sort of work, ain't you?"

Teddy drew back his coat far enough to show Dog the shoulder holster and the Colt Lightning that hung from it.

"My birth certificate," he said, and let the coat fall over the rig again before walking out.

He went and sent a telegram to George Bangs.

*Have arrived in Dodge this day. Met with one of the principals. Will begin work immediately.*

*T. Blue.*

The room he took at the Dodge House overlooked Front Street. It had a good bed, tall ceiling, two windows and a back stairway. He unpacked his valise, placing his extra shirts in the top drawer of the bureau that stood against one wall. Socks too. He placed his razor atop the bureau next to the washbasin. This complete, he felt the unsettling sense of being without companionship for the first time since leaving Mexico. He wondered how John was making out.

The light outside was a mixture of sunlight and grayish blue, the sky uncertain whether it was bringing in a storm or something less troublesome. He noticed a hardware store across the street with the words GUNS AMMUNITION KNIVES painted in large black letters on an oversize wooden rifle mounted on a pole out front. Next to the hardware was a butcher shop with two men in white aprons standing out front talking and smoking cigarettes. Their white aprons had bloodstains on them. A wagon pulled up and one of them went inside and came back out again with a slab of beef over his shoulder that he heaved into the back of the wagon, his cigarette dangling from his mouth.

From his vantage point, Teddy could see where the town ended and the prairies began. And as far as he could see, there wasn't a distraction for the eye except one thing: a cemetery. There was always a cemetery, a place to bury the dead, both the good and bad together. Death made everyone equal—the same as Sam Colt's pistols. The graveyard looked like a garden of wooden crosses and stone markers. It looked somehow out of place. Farther out still, he could see a lone tree that had been lightning struck, whose branches and trunk were black.

Teddy wondered what it was that possessed the first man to have stopped in this place. To say to himself, I think I'll start a town here.

*The son of a bitch must have busted an axle on his wagon and just couldn't go any farther.* For there was no indication why this particular latitude and longitude would attract a man other than by sheer accident.

Teddy pulled off his boots and stretched out on the bed.

There wasn't much use to go looking for trouble until after dark—not if Dodge was like every other frontier town he'd ever been in.

Darkness and trouble just naturally went together, and so too did the men who feasted upon them. Assassins and such.

# Chapter 5

The weather had cleared after two stormy days. Sun broke through the treacherous skies warm enough to melt the ice that coated the prairies and Dodge. Bat and Ed had grown restless and were itching to get after Dirty Dave Rudabaugh.

During the stormy lull, Bat had told Ed about Dog Kelly's suspicions that there were going to be some serious attempts on their lives and that he had further sent for a Pinkerton.

Ed said, "I reckon we can handle ourselves."

"That's what I told Dog Kelly."

"Maybe we ought to just cross over them tracks and shoot every son of a bitch looks cross-eyed at us."

"That would sure put the word out we meant business and weren't going to run scared."

"Hell, I don't care if Dog sends for the goddamn United States Cavalry."

"At least what's left of 'em after that Custer debacle," Bat said.

They were saddling their mounts with high hopes of running Dirty Dave to ground this time.

"Yeah," Ed said. "I guess he learned them Cheyenne and Sioux weren't so easily whipped."

Bat's smile was sardonic; he'd known Custer and didn't care for him much. Most like Custer—full of bluster and overly confident—ended up in early graves.

"You ever stop to think," Ed said, tying his soogins to the back of his saddle, "that if it weren't for certain fellers who figured they could get away with just about anything, me and you wouldn't have a job?"

"There will always be those types, Brother Ed. I just wish we didn't have to ride so far to bring some of 'em to justice."

"I don't guess Dirty Dave and his type is just going to ride into town and give himself up for our convenience, do you?"

"No. But it would sure be considerate of him if he did."

Ed came around and put a foot in a stirrup and said, "You reckon we're still going to need these oilskins?"

"I don't feel any rain in me, so I guess we might not. But we better wear mackinaws, it could turn cold enough to maybe snow. Weather out on these prairies is moodier than most women."

"Maybe we can get our money back from Harry for 'em. We only wore 'em just that once."

Bat looked at him, said, "You always was more Scotch than me."

They had ridden out of Dodge the very day the train carrying the Pinkerton man arrived.

Bat was still irked that Dog Kelly had seen it necessary to hire a Pinkerton in the first place. "He must think we can't handle ourselves in a pistol fight if it comes down to it," Bat said as they rode along.

"I may be more Scotch than you, but you was always a hotter head than me," Ed said.

They rode toward Liberal, Bat saying about Dirty Dave and his confederates, "Their ilk is of a lazy nature and they may well hang around in a place like Liberal instead of riding all the way down to the pistol barrel of Oklahoma."

Ed did not dispute Bat's instinct for tracking or for knowing a man's nature—especially the nature of outlaws. The brothers, along with their other sibling, Jim, had hunted plenty of buffalo when there were still buffalo to be hunted, and it was Bat who always found the largest and fattest herds. Ed reckoned Bat could track a fish through water if he set his mind to it. And it was Bat who talked him into becoming a peace officer, Bat saying, "We don't have to be geniuses to outwit most of the lawbreakers, we just have to be brave."

They saw a pair of red-tailed hawks wheeling through the skies.

"It's like they're dancing," Bat said.

"I wish sometimes I had wings so I could get places faster."

"I don't want to end up dead someday out in this country, do you?"

Ed looked at his brother. He'd never thought much about death, being the young man that he was. "I don't guess it makes a difference to me where I end up dead at. Dead's dead, far as I'm concerned. I reckon being dead in Kansas is about like being dead anywhere else."

"That's not what I'm referring to. I'd like to believe that I have more of a future to me than ending up in some prairie grave and never making a real name for myself. I'd like to do something bold before it's all said and done, wouldn't you?"

"I'd settle just for meeting a pretty gal and getting married and maybe wear a fine suit and become president of a bank or something. This is a good-enough place for young fellers like us to make a name for ourselves—to have a future in, Bat."

They rode for a good long way, thinking about life on those prairies, future prospects, death, living, and red-tailed hawks. Then they realized how far they'd ridden and what lay just ahead of them.

"Let's not ride past the Dutchman's," Ed said. "I don't want to have to see that place and be reminded of what we found there."

"We'll ride wide of it."

They could still see those shadowy lumps inside the soddy, the small ones and those of the Dutchman slumped there at the table and his wife lying on the small bed.

They rode on in silence for a time after they knew they'd well skirted the Dutchman's.

"You ever bed that Foster woman?" Ed said at last.

Bat blinked.

"Lydia, the one who ran the hat shop?"

"No, the schoolteacher back in Sedgewick."

"Why would you ask me something like that?"

"I have always just been curious is all."

"You?"

"No, she was a lot older'n me. I thought about it, but I never did."

"Well, I never did either."

"I think she had eyes for you."

"I never had any for her."

"She might have been all right, the more I think about it."

"I don't see how you could think about something like that."

"She had a nice way about her, even though she wasn't very attractive, if you know what I mean. I bet she was close to forty, wouldn't you say?"

Bat chose not to think about old schoolteachers he and Ed had been taught by and attributed Ed's meandering mind to the sheer boredom that comes with long rides across featureless land. Bat would rather concentrate on the job at hand: catching Dirty Dave Rudabaugh.

They arrived in Liberal well past dark their third day out. They had spotted that little town by the lights of its saloons, twinkling in the distance, and were glad to finally see it. They rode on in and tied off at the first liquor establishment they came to: a place called Zel's.

Ed stopped short of going in, said, "How you want to take 'em when we find 'em?"

Bat was two years younger than his brother, but Ed most generally deferred to Bat on matters of confronting trouble. Bat was fearless.

"We'll ask them to disarm, tell 'em we're arresting 'em for the robbery. Like we'd do with anybody."

"And if they don't go easily?"

"You still got your mind on pussy?"

"No, why do you ask?"

"Because you're talking like we never done this before, like you got your head somewhere else."

"I just didn't know if you wanted to shoot Dave if it come to it. He's not that bad a sort, really—just stupid and dirty."

"We'll leave it up to him if he wants us to shoot him or not. How's that?"

"That's fine by me."

They went in, their hands inside their coat pockets where they carried their pistols. They'd done this sort of work before, like Bat had said.

The air was smoky, and there was a good deal of drinking and gambling and conversation going on. Men stood along the bar, others sat at tables, and some played roulette and some buck the tiger and some stud poker.

Bat and Ed ordered whiskeys to warm their

blood and get it going in the right way in their veins, and they looked around cautiously to see if Dirty Dave Rudabaugh was among the clientele. They didn't see him.

"What now?" Ed said.

"I swear, you still got your mind on that old schoolmarm. Drink up and let's go."

They walked down to the next saloon and went in and didn't see Dave there either. They continued their search for him, and when they walked into the fourth liquor parlor, there he was, sitting at a table with three others: men in slouch hats. Low types, anybody could see by their manner of dress.

"That's him," Bat said, nodding to Ed as they walked to the bar.

"Four of 'em," Ed said.

"I can count."

"Which side you want?"

"It don't matter."

"I'll take the right side then."

"Okay."

"Now?'

"No, let's have another whiskey first."

"It might make you a little slow."

"It ain't never before. Besides, if things go bad, it might be the last chance I get to take a drink."

"Hell, I guess I never thought about it that way."

They ordered two whiskeys, drank them while watching Dave and his bunch in the back bar mirror. There was several mounted heads of buffalo over the bar with lonesome glass eyes staring down on the unsuspecting patrons. Ed was looking at them.

"You remember old Bill Jackson?" Ed said.

"What about him?"

"How he had that glass eye . . ."

"So?"

Ed pointed with his chin up to the mounted heads.

"Wonder where all them glass eyes come from?"

"Jesus," Bat said. "Let's go do this."

Dave was saying something to one of the men at his table when Bat stepped out of the shadows with a Colt Peacemaker in his hand and said, "Rudabaugh, I've come to arrest you and these others for robbing the Katy flier."

Then Ed stepped out of the shadows from Dave's right and showed him the Smith and Wesson in his hand, and showed it to the others too.

"I expect you boys know how this is supposed to work."

Dirty Dave had grimy features, like he'd been down in a pit shoveling dirt all day.

"You fucking Mastersons just don't quit, do you?"

"No, we don't," Bat said.

Dave looked at his companions, said, "I told you boys we should have kept riding till we crossed the damn state line."

Bat ordered them to stand with their hands up.

"Slow," Ed reminded them as they scraped back their chairs.

One moved too fast to suit Bat and he stepped in close and brought the barrel of his pistol down hard enough to flatten the crown of the man's hat and the skull that rested under it, and knocked the man senseless.

"Next one gets shot. Hell, it will be a lot less trouble if you boys just provoke us into shooting all of you. We'll rent a wagon and haul your carcasses back like a load of wood."

"Jeez Christ, boys," Dave moaned, "we've had it."

Bat tossed a bucket of beer on the one he'd coldcocked and ordered the others to help him to his feet. Once they marched outside, Ed hauled leg and wrist irons from his saddle pockets and tossed them at the feet of the prisoners. "Put 'em on, boys. Do it careful, like they were snakes you handling, 'cause brother Bat here gets nervous when felons move too quick." They covered the four with their pistols until they'd snapped on the irons, then marched them in a shuffling gait down to the local law-enforcement office.

A big-bellied deputy locked them in a cell when Ed and Bat explained the situation.

"We'll come and pick 'em up in the morning," Bat said.

Back out on the street again, they found a hotel and rented a room and went up and pulled off their boots, both weary from the long ride they'd

had and the thought of what a long ride it would
be to return to Dodge.

Ed flopped down on the bed and said, "I'm
about wore to a nub."

Bat took a small book from his pocket—a collection of poetry by Sir Walter Raleigh—and
opened it as he took a seat by the lamp.

"You always had a more curious mind than
me," Ed said, feeling the burn behind his eyes.

Bat hardly seemed to acknowledge his brother
as he read *On the Life of a Man* and was particu-
larly struck by some of the lines: *What is our life?
A play of passion . . . when we are drest for this
short Comedy . . .*

In the background he could hear Ed's snores.
Darkness, complete and black as hell, lay outside
the window.

*Our graves that hide us from the searching Sun,
Are like drawne curtaynes when the play is
done . . .*

But he took a deep breath and sighed. Took
from his other pocket the Peacemaker and laid it
on the nightstand, and next to it the book of po-
ems as his thoughts turned over images of graves
hid from the searching sun and the passionate life
he was sure somehow he was not quite living.

Brother Ed was asleep as the dead.

*We were boys once, and now we're men,*
thought Bat.

He felt fully alone in the world, and sleep did
not come so easily.

## Chapter 6

------ ◆ ------

Gunshots announced night had fallen in Dodge. Teddy rose from the bed and went to the window and looked out. He saw no bodies lying on the streets. It was a good sign.

He slipped on the shoulder rig with the Colt Lightning, then his coat and hat and went out. On the sidewalk in front of the hotel, the town north of the tracks seemed asleep, the shops locked, few pedestrians. He walked down toward the south end of town, where Dog Kelly said the rumors and the men possibly behind the rumors to kill the Mastersons ran the pleasure trade.

Once he reached the tracks he crossed them, and the quiet world slipped away. The saloons were in full swing. He did a quick count of half a dozen of them either side of the street. He drifted into the first one he came to, The Paris Club. There wasn't anything French about it other than the name. It looked like every other saloon he'd ever been in: full of loud men and other noises, cigar smoke and bad smells. He worked his way to the bar and ordered a short whiskey and took his time with it.

When he finished and the barkeep came over again, Teddy asked to talk to the owner, asked for him by name—Frenchy LeBreck—the name Dog Kelly had given him earlier.

"That's him over to the faro bank," the barkeep said.

"Bring me a beer," Teddy said.

Teddy waited nearly an hour before LeBreck took his leave of the faro bank and drifted over to the bar.

"My name's Blue," Teddy said, "I'd like a private word with you."

LeBreck was a short wiry man with eyebrows that looked like they'd grown together, fierce hawkish eyes.

"A possible business proposition," Teddy said when he saw LeBreck's hesitation.

LeBreck motioned for him to walk to the end of the bar. Once done, LeBreck said, "What sort of proposition?" The accent was Cajun if anything, Teddy surmised.

"I'm a man who does things for a price," Teddy said.

"What sort of things, eh?"

"Things most other men won't do."

LeBreck placed both hands on top of the bar, flat.

"I've no time to talk foolishness, *mon ami*."

"Like I said, my name's Blue, Teddy Blue, and

I'm staying at the Dodge House, room twelve."
Teddy drew the front of his coat open far enough
for LeBreck to get a look at the gun, then let it fall
closed again.

LeBreck's eyes met his.

"What makes you think—"

"There's always someone in need of the type of
work I do. If not you, maybe somebody you
know. I'm just putting the word around."

LeBreck said, "I don't know anything about
what you're talking about," and walked away.

The seed was planted. It was enough—time to
move on.

He crossed the street to the Black Cat, one of
the other three places Dog Kelly had mentioned.
Aside from being a little narrower, you couldn't
tell this saloon from the first. This time, when he
asked for the owner, the big man tending bar said,
"I'd be him. Angus Bush."

Teddy dropped a silver dollar on the bar, ordered a cocktail.

"Fancy drink, don't get too many calls for
'em," Angus Bush said, mixing up the drink and
setting it on the oak. "Fact is, the only other man
I ever met who drank them regular was Wild Bill
Hickok. Had me a place in Abilene a few years
back when he was the law there. He'd come in just
about every night and order a cocktail."

"He's dead, you know."

"Yes, so I've heard." Angus Bush looked at
Teddy suspiciously. "Have we met?"

Teddy said, "I think you'd remembered if we had."

Angus Bush, unlike Frenchy LeBreck, was a huge barrel-chested man with hands like small hams. His wiry beard looked like a tangle of rusted wire.

"What'd you say your name was?"

"I didn't, but it's Blue, Teddy Blue."

Teddy could see Bush turning the name over in his mind, trying to dredge up a memory that he wouldn't find.

"Just to let you know," Teddy said. "I'm available for certain kinds of work."

"And what kinds would that be?"

Teddy fingered back the front of his coat enough to give Angus Bush a look at the iron he carried in the shoulder rig.

"That kind," he said.

"I see."

"In case you hear of anything, I'd appreciate it," Teddy said, dropping another dollar on the bar. "I'm staying at the Dodge House, room twelve."

He could feel Angus Bush's stare on his shoulder blades as he walked out, leaving the cocktail untouched on the bar.

He hit a couple more places before coming to the Silk Garter, a much larger establishment than the others—more garish. There was loud piano music coming from inside. Teddy could see the place was doing a good business. In a short time he could see why: There were twice as many saloon girls working the Garter as there were in the other places.

Two roulette tables, a faro bank, buck the tiger, and chuck-a-luck games, as well as regular poker were heavily played. A long bar took up all of one wall.

Teddy asked one of the three bartenders for Bone Butcher Swain.

"He's busy," the man said.

"I'd like to talk to him."

"He won't allow himself being disturbed when he's with the Rose."

"The Rose?"

"The Rose of Cimarron."

"When might he be available?"

"Hard to say. Sometimes its an all-nighter, know what I mean?" the barkeep said with a sly wink.

"Yeah, I know what you mean. I'll come back around tomorrow."

"You want a drink?"

"No."

The barkeep looked him over, then moved down to another patron.

Teddy felt hunger gnawing at his ribs, realized he hadn't eaten in a long time. When he left the Garter, he walked back up across the tracks to the Wright House for dinner. It's where he met the woman, Mae.

\* \* \*

She had hair like the morning sun and eyes blue as a clear Kansas sky and he knew he should ignore those two attributes when she waited on his table, but he could not. Their eyes met and held—her clear blue ones, his dark serious ones.

He mused over the menu written in chalk on a board there on the wall, but stealing glances at her in between, asking questions like how was the beef and so forth, anything to engage her in conversation.

"You don't have to try so hard," she said.

"I don't know what you mean."

"I think you do."

He smiled.

"If you don't order something I'm going to have to wait on someone else," she said.

So he ordered the beef with roasted potatoes and a cup of coffee, and she brought him the coffee first and he said thank you and she looked at him again and said, "I haven't seen you in here before."

"I just got into town this afternoon."

"Oh," she said, and he could hear the wariness in her voice.

She went off to wait on others and returned in fifteen minutes with his steak and set the plate before him and asked if there was anything else he needed.

"Not right this moment, but I might have some dessert when I'm finished. And, some more coffee when you get a chance."

"Surely," she said. He liked the aloof way she said it, but with a smile in her eyes.

He couldn't say what it was about her that attracted him apart from the obvious: that she was good-looking. It was more than just the fact that she was pretty.

He ate slowly so he could observe her, to see how many times she might come over and refill his coffee cup or glance in his direction. She seemed to pay him no greater attention than anyone else and he felt a little disappointed.

Finally he finished and pushed his plate away and took out his makings and rolled himself a cigarette and lit it.

She came to take his plate and he said, "I think I'll try the apple pie."

She went off and came back again in a few minutes with a plate of pie and set it before him and said, "I've heard it's excellent."

"We could split it," he said.

A smile played at the edges of her mouth. "I'm not really allowed to socialize," she said. "The boss doesn't want us to engage with the customers."

"How else are you supposed to know what they want?"

"You know quite well what I mean."

"I apologize," he said. She walked away. He finished the pie and washed the last of it down with the coffee still warm in his cup and stood. He left a dollar tip on the table next to the cup.

He settled his Stetson down on his head and

headed for the door. She was waiting on a couple when he walked past.

"I get off in an hour," she said.

"I'll wait for you outside."

He saw the couple smile.

It was the slowest damn hour he remembered having to wait. He thought about John Sears in that time and smoked several more cigarettes and felt the night around him as people came and went. Then at last the lights started going out inside the restaurant and suddenly there she was.

"My name is Mae," she said. "Mae Simmons."

"Teddy Blue," he said. "Can I walk you home?"

"I'm staying at Caldwell's Boarding House. It's where most of the single girls stay," she said. "But we don't need to go straight there. I like to walk for a time, if you wouldn't mind. Just to see the stars . . ."

"Then let's just walk," he said.

They walked out toward the edge of town. He could hardly hear her footsteps on the boards.

"Where did you come from?" she asked.

"Down in Mexico, but before that, Chicago."

"Really? You're a man who gets around a lot."

"Yes, I reckon so. What about you?"

"I came here from Canada."

"Tell me how you managed to make your way to Dodge," he said.

"Oh, it's such an odd and probably boring story."

"I've got all night, Mae."

So she told him about the husband who'd brought her down from Canada—his name was Jim Belt. She said he had been a good man except for one weakness—gambling—and that it had cost him his life. This happened a year ago, she said.

"How come you stayed? Dodge doesn't seem like much of a town for a young widow."

"My late husband didn't leave an estate," she said. "I had to work. I'm saving every spare nickel, knowing that someday I will be able to leave here and start a new life. I'm not exactly sure where I want to go when I do leave, but I'll be ready when the time comes.

"You said your husband's last name was Belt?"

"I took back my maiden name after he died. There was no reason to keep it, we'd only been married two years—two very bad years, when I think back on it."

They stood there at the very edge of town, and even though the night was cold it was clear and they could see a million stars and a new moon so full and bright it looked like they could almost walk up to it and put their hands on it.

"I love to imagine what it would be like to go to the moon," she said. "To go any place exotic and far away."

Something about her voice—a touch of sadness, perhaps—caused him to think of Anne.

"What is it?" she said. He hadn't realized how long he'd fallen silent.

"I was just thinking about another woman I know who also lost her husband last year."

"Someone you were in love with?"

He looked at her. "Why would you think that?"

"Just the way you sounded."

And then an odd thing happened. A horse, unsaddled, ran across the prairie. At that distance and under the moon's light, the horse looked like a silver shadow.

"Look," she said.

And for several moments after the horse passed from view they could hear the thud of its hooves. Then silence reclaimed the prairie.

"How strange," she said.

"Perhaps it is some sort of sign."

She drew her capote closer around her shoulders. "It's getting cold," she said. "We should start back."

They walked along without speaking until they reached the front of the boarding house where she was staying.

"This is it," she said.

"Thank you for the walk, Mae."

"Teddy . . ."

"Yes?"

It was as though she wanted to ask him something important. He waited but she said, "Oh, nothing."

"I know it must seem to you like we're strangers, Mae. But there's something about you that makes me feel as though I've known you for longer than just a few hours."

"I feel it too."

Somewhere off in the darkness they heard dogs barking.

"I'd like to go for another walk sometime," he said.

"So would I . . . Good night."

He waited until she'd gone inside the house before starting back to his room at the hotel. He wasn't quite sure what to feel toward her, considering he still had deep feelings for Anne and lingering ones for Kathleen. It felt a lot like betrayal somehow, to have feelings for yet another woman.

The moon stood high over Dodge now and the town seemed to stand defiant and ready for the worst to happen. It was as though the town in its starkness shouted silently: *I will swallow your whiskey and gunshots and empty your pockets. I will tempt you with whores and fill you with sin and bury you with your boots still on and not look back. And a thousand moons will rise and fall over your graves and I will still be here.*

He could not help but feel some unknown force had brought him and the woman together for a reason that none of them would understand until it became a *fait accompli*.

John probably would have said, "Fuck all that thinking, son. Just let things be as they are and don't question none of it."

John would have been right.

# Chapter 7

The Pepper twins were arguing over who should get first turn with Mosely's wife in the back of the wagon when Two Bits shot them.

Mosely was sitting on a bucket shivering from the tremors brought on by all the snakehead whiskey he'd drank that morning and all the mornings up until that morning. Mosely's wife waited impatiently for the twins to come to some decision. It was cold there in the back of the wagon.

"Mosely, tell them young'ns to hurry it up," she called. Every time she spoke his name, Mosely's headache seemed to grow worse.

*Lord, how did I ever sink so low in life as to be a drunk and a pimp for my own wife?* he wondered achingly. It had been a pretty morning right up until Two Bits shot the brothers. Mosely had camped by a stream outside of Red Mountain—just far enough outside of the town to avoid violating any pandering laws the town might have, or any sheriffs it might have to enforce pandering laws if there were any. Mosely had once been a student of the law before he fell into the clutches of the demon rum, as Mosely's wife called it.

Everything about his current situation seemed to Mosely surreal, like a real bad dream that just kept playing over and over in his head. He was half tempted to shoot himself just to see if it was a dream. But even attempted suicide seemed too large a task for Mosely that particular morning. And besides, he had no bullets for the rusty revolver in his belt.

It was Mosely's wife who had first suggested how they could make a little money. At first he protested. It seemed unseemly, even for a man who'd sunk to Mosely's condition, to be pimping for his own wife.

He said as much. She laughed, said to him, "Well, are we going to eat dirt to stay alive, or do you have some better plan?" Mosely's wife could be harsh when she wanted to be.

It was true; Mosely had not a single nickel to his name to buy so much as a loaf of bread, and had traded away everything he'd owned of value for liquor except the wagon and the old horse that pulled it, and judging the way the horse had been acting lately, Mosely was sure that the horse was not long for this world either.

"I can leave you and let you fend for yourself, Mosely," she said. "I can leave you out here in this wilderness to die a slow and terrible death, or you can swallow that foolish pride of yours along with the last few drops of that poison you call liquor and overlook what it is I have to do. It's your choice, Mosely."

He could not but conclude that she did love him, even if her reason for doing so escaped him. He wasn't sure if he loved her, but he had no one else to care for him.

Bernard, one of the twins, was arguing that since he was paying for both of them he should go first with Mosely's wife. Hank, the other one, reasoned that it was he who'd done the negotiating with Mosely and got him down to a price that matched the amount in their pockets, and that he ought to go first.

Mosely had met his wife in a Leadville whorehouse several years previous. She was so pretty he stole her in the middle of the night. She'd put up little protest. Mosely had been wild back in those days—wild and bold and a regular rootin' tootin' cowboy of the first order. Now he just felt old and foolish.

"We'll flip a coin for it," one of the twins said. Mosely had forgotten which one was Bernard and which was Hank, not that it mattered. He thought it was Hank who suggested flipping a coin. What little Mosely knew about them was that they were a rich cattleman's progeny who had too much time on their hands and more money in their pockets than boys their age should be entitled to. This much he'd learned about them the first time they visited his camp and paid for the privilege of consorting with Mosely's wife. This event having taken place a week previous. They had ridden in two more times, not counting this day.

The only thing that pleased Mosely about the boys was that they always brought along a bottle of store-bought whiskey, which beat hell out of the homemade snakehead Mosely could afford. Mosely called it forty-rod liquor, what the boys brought. It had such a kick to it, it would knock a man forty rods.

"You had her first last time," one of the twins said. Maybe Bernard.

"Ah shit, that don't mean nothing, let's ask her which one of us she wants to go first."

"Fair enough."

"Ma'am," one of them said into the back of the wagon, "which one of us would you prefer to go first?"

"I don't give a coon's ass which," she said in a loud impatient voice. "Let's just get on with it, I've got gooseflesh." The boys sniggered, because they'd been into the forty-rod too.

Mosely was thinking how pretty his wife had been when he met her, how pretty and sweet and thin she was. She was like a waif, an angel, a fairy, he reflected. She was so light he could carry her in one arm, and did. But, she'd started letting herself go after Mosely married her. She had grown thick and moon-faced and her temperament had gotten bad as well. He figured the laudanum she'd come to love so much had something to do with it.

A single raindrop fell from the overcast sky and

thunked Mosely on the tip of his nose. He looked up, thought, *Christ, it's going to rain on me.*

The twins were fumbling around in the pockets of their britches for a coin to flip to see who would go first with Mosely's wife. Finally one of them came up with one, said, "Call it," and flipped what looked like to Mosely a perfectly shiny standing Liberty silver dollar into the air. And when it came down, the boy who flipped it caught it and slapped it atop his left wrist just before the other boy said, "Heads."

That was exactly when Two Bits shot the one who caught the coin.

The bullet almost knocked him out of his boots. There was a long frozen moment when nobody moved or said anything except Mosely's wife from back of the wagon.

"What the hell was that, thunder?"

The shot boy lay there with his legs jerking like a frog that had been gigged. He lay atop what looked like a whole bucket of blood flowing out from underneath him.

Then Two Bits shot the other boy and the shot about knocked him out of his boots as well, flung him against the side of the wagon and he collapsed like a rag doll.

"It's the Rapture!" Mosely screamed. He'd read about the Rapture in the Bible—Book of Revelations—though he hardly understood most of it except for the part where the world would end in fire and brimstone and some would be taken up into heaven and others would be left behind. Or something like that.

Mosely reached for the whiskey bottle. He could see there was still a swallow's worth that needed drinking. Mosely's wife's head popped out of the back of the wagon. She saw first the one twin then the other.

"Mosely, did you shoot them boys out of jealousy?"

"No," Mosely said.

She was sure that Mosely had shot them and it filled her with a sense of anger and love for him. Anger because he'd shot two perfectly good customers, and love because only an extremely jealous man would go to such extremes to protect his wife's honor, especially if she had no honor to protect.

"Well, I ought to be mad at you," Mosely's wife said, exiting the back of the wagon. She'd wrapped her gooseflesh in an old moth-riddled quilt. "I just wish there was another way to show your displeasure other than shooting them boys, Mosely."

"I didn't shoot them," Mosely said.

"Who did, if you didn't?"

"He did," Mosely said, pointing to the man walking up from a little stand of pine trees. He was carrying a big bore rifle and he had a pair of pistols stuck inside his belt and he looked scraggly in the face and everywhere under his hat.

"You going to shoot us too?" Mosely asked when the man got close enough.

"No, I ain't going to shoot you," the man said.

"Why'd you shoot them nice boys," Mosely's wife said, "if you ain't a dirty killer and ain't planning on killing Mosely and me too?"

"I shot 'em because I got paid to shoot 'em," the man said. "Nobody's paid me to shoot either of you. Unless you want to pay me."

"I ain't got even a nickel to my name," Mosely said.

"Then I guess you won't get shot today," the man said. He looked Mosely's wife over real hard. She looked him over real hard as well.

"Those were customers of mine you shot," Mosely's wife said.

"Customers?" The man looked from her to Mosely. "You mean . . ." the man started to say.

Mosely just looked off toward some mountains he could see in the distance. They had snow on their peaks. He felt as cold inside his heart as he thought that snow was cold.

"Well," the man said to Mosely's wife. "I guess there wouldn't be nobody to say anything if you wanted to take the money out of those boys' pockets."

"You mean rob the dead?"

"Well, it don't look like that one feller is quite yet, but he will be soon."

Mosely sat there watching his once sweet and

slender wife waddle over and pick clean the wallets of the twins, giving each a little kiss on the forehead as she sobbed loudly, "I'm sorry, boys, but you won't be needing this, and me and Mosely will. I just wish you hadn't wasted so much time arguing over who would go first and would have got to take your pleasure one last time before this tragic thing happened to you . . ."

"She always carry on so?" the man said. "I'm Two Bits, by the way."

"I'm Mosely," Mosely said, and, "She didn't use to. She use to be sweet and kind of on the quiet side."

"Well, I guess I'll be getting on," Two Bits said.

"Mind I ask you who it was who paid you to shoot them boys?" Mosely said. "Except for their foolishness, they seemed like rather nice boys."

"Somebody who wanted 'em dead," Two Bits said. "You want anybody dead you're willing to pay for?"

Mosely looked toward his wife who was counting out the money she'd taken from the bloody wallets of the twins.

"No, I don't reckon," Mosely said. "And even if I did, like I said before, I don't have a nickel to my name."

Two Bits looked at Mosely's wife.

"How about you?" he said. "Anybody you want to pay me to shoot dead now that you've come into some money?"

Mosely's wife looked at Mosely. She shook her head.

"Well, then I'll be getting on," Two Bits said again. "I've got other work waiting for me down in Kansas. Seems like when it rains jobs, it pours 'em."

They watched him go off into the trees.

"There's almost forty dollars here," Mosely's wife said.

"I wouldn't care if it were a thousand," Mosely said. "I don't feel good about what happened. I feel near sick."

"Maybe we should get down on our knees and pray," Mosely's wife said. "I think maybe this is a sign for you to stop drinking and me to stop whoring. I think God is giving us a second chance, Mosely."

Mosely looked at that last little bit of liquor in the bottom of the bottle the twins had brought with them. It looked like temptation, those last few drops of liquor. It looked just like wet brown temptation, and so too did that silver dollar lying by the outstretched hand of the dead boy. Winking as it was in the morning sun, just like a temptress's eye—winking at Mosely, to where he couldn't stand it anymore and went and picked it up and put it into his pocket.

"I reckon you could be right," Mosely said to his wife. "It could be a sign of some sort telling us to repent."

Mosely looked at his wife and she looked at him. They both knew that their hearts were in the right place, but that it might be a lot harder road to travel than it seemed. Then they looked at the dead twins and knew salvation wasn't a thing easily had.

A bluebird chirped merrily in the top of a tree.

## Chapter 8

————◆————

Dog Kelly arrived almost with the sun. Early. Teddy opened the door and there Dog was standing under his slightly crushed stovepipe hat, still wearing the same dusty swallowtail coat and looking hollow-eyed.

"How'd you make out in your investigation last night?" Dog said.

"I made the rounds south of the tracks. I put the word out I was a gun for hire. Figured it was a good ploy."

"Smart," Dog Kelly said. "I should have thought of that ploy myself." Dog wasn't exactly sure what the word *ploy* meant, but figured it had something to do with the Pinkerton man's overall plan.

"Bat and Ed is back in town. They come in late last night."

"They find the men they were after?"

"They did."

"Good for them."

"Not so good. Dirty Dave and his bunch busted out of the jail down in Liberal after Bat and Ed locked 'em up down there. Dug their way out with spoons. Spoons! Goddamn, what sort of piss-poor jail they got down there, I says to Bat when he told me. Bat says, just that, piss poor, walls made out of mud. That's twice they went after them boys and twice they missed 'em."

"Bad luck," said Teddy over his shoulder as he pulled a clean shirt from the drawer of the bureau. "When are you going to introduce me to Bat and Ed?"

"Bat's having coffee down to the Lone Star. Ed ain't as early a riser."

"What time is it?"

Dog Kelly took a big pocket watch from his vest pocket and snapped open the case. "Almost seven in the morning."

"You don't look like you got any shuteye."

"I don't sleep much. Find it to be a lot like death, sleeping is . . . Don't care for it at all."

Teddy pulled on his coat and took his hat off a hook on the back of the door and they walked down the stairs and out the front door. Sun was just breaking through a bank of clouds far off to the east. The winter-brown prairies looked golden in the light. Dog Kelly was a heavy walker; his boot heels clunked hard on the boardwalk. He wasn't that big of a man, but the way he walked made him sound like he was.

The Lone Star was empty except for Bat, sitting at a table drinking a cup of coffee, and his sibling,

Jim, stocking shelves from a crate of whiskey arrived a few minutes earlier.

Bat looked up when Dog and Teddy entered. Jim did not.

Bat's face was saturnine. He let his gaze fall on Teddy and Dog without any change of expression.

"This is Sheriff Masterson," Dog said. "And this is Teddy Blue, the Pinkerton I sent for."

Bat nodded toward the chair opposite him, said, "Take a seat."

Dog Kelly went to the end of the bar and filled two tin cups with coffee from a pot heating on a woodburner in the corner.

"We've met before, haven't we?" Bat said.

"In Cheyenne last year," Teddy said. Bat's features relaxed a little.

"Yes, I remember now, you killed Hank Rain . . . I was there, saw the whole thing go down."

"It was an unfortunate incident," Teddy said, just as Dog Kelly set the cups down on the table.

"You damn right it was unfortunate," Bat said. "For Hank Rain."

"Killing's not my game."

"Killing's not your game?"

"No."

"Then what are you doing working as a Pinkerton? And why'd you come to a hellhole like Dodge?"

"It's a long story. Suffice it to say, I go where I'm told."

Dog made a mental note of the word *suffice*. He had an old dictionary behind the bar at his establishment, weighing, he guessed, ten pounds—yellowing pages, some missing. He'd look up *suffice* first chance he got.

"You don't strike me as the sort to just go where you're told."

"We can sit and debate what sort of man I am if you want, but that's not what I think the mayor here is paying for."

Bat looked at Dog, who was blowing the steam off his coffee.

"Hotter'n a stove lid," Dog said. "Tastes about like it too."

"They got coffee places other than mine," Bat said. "You don't have to drink it here."

"Look, Sheriff, I know you're not too damn happy about my presence here, but Mayor Kelly's right about one thing; nobody knows me here, and I can possibly learn information neither of you can about this conspiracy."

"Conspiracy, huh?"

"Whatever you choose to call it."

"He's right, Bat," Dog said. "Let him do his job, let me do mine and that way you and Ed can do yours."

"I've nothing against you personally, Mr. Blue. I just don't need a nursemaid and neither does Ed."

"I never thought you did. Tell you what, let me try and help you find out who the men are who want to assassinate you and your brother, and you can handle them any way you deem fit. How's that?"

"It's a free country, where a man can do what he wants, ain't that what they say?"

"That's what they say."

Bat sipped some more of his coffee. Teddy gauged Bat and Jim to be close in age, only Bat looked like he had a lot more frontier in him than most that age.

"Just to let you know," Teddy said. "I put the word around south of the tracks I'm a gun for hire. The hope being of course that whoever wants you dead will hire me to kill you."

Bat looked at him with those dark sad eyes from under the bowler.

"Make you a deal," Bat said.

"What's that?"

"Go three rounds with me in the ring. If you're still on your feet at the end, I'll shake your hand and give you my full cooperation."

"I'm not a fighter."

"You damn well better become one if you intend on staying in Dodge."

"Okay," Teddy said. "Set it up."

Bat smiled, Dog did too.

"Noon, right here. We'll clear the floor and I'll have Jim put up some ropes for a ring."

"I'll keep the time," Dog said.

"And I'm guessing you'll take bets too," Teddy said.

"Of course," Dog said. "It wouldn't be no fight without bets laid down."

Teddy stood and said, "See you at noon, Mr. Masterson."

"You whip my ass, you can call me Bat, Detective Blue."

Teddy could see that Bat Masterson, though not a tall man, was solid as a stump all over. Still, it was an opportunity to show the rest of the town that he and Bat, and by proxy the other Masterson brothers, were at odds over something.

"Tell you what, Mayor," Teddy said. "Pass the word around while you're promoting the fight and laying down bets it's some sort of grudge match."

Dog smiled and Teddy thought maybe he saw a half smile of recognition on Bat's face as well.

"I'll do her, boy, I'll play her up big," Dog said enthusiastically.

Teddy walked over to the Wright House after he left the Lone Star. Mae was there. He could see her waiting tables through the plate glass. He went in and took a seat. She saw him and came over.

"You must put in a long day," he said.

"Every day. It helps me save my money faster, working long hours. Breakfast?"

"Of course. Make it a big one, I've got to fist-fight a fellow in a few hours and will need my strength."

She looked at him askance, saw the slight grin playing at his mouth.

"You like boxing matches, Mae?"

"I don't care for any sort of violence," she said.

"I do this right, there won't be that much violence to it."

"Don't count on me being in the audience."

"Flapjacks," Teddy said. "Lots of 'em and several slices of fried ham too."

She went away and came back later with his meal and set it before him and poured him coffee and stood for a moment watching him eat.

"What?" he said.

She shook her head.

"Men . . ." she said, and walked away.

Noon found him back in the Lone Star, a lot more crowded now than earlier. Men lined the walls. A hasty ring of ropes tied to support posts and chairs had been constructed. Every eye fell on Teddy when he walked through the doors. Dog rushed up to greet him.

"I see you got the word out," Teddy said.

"This time of year, things is slow, folks would pay to see a good spitting match, but this is even better."

Teddy went over to a chair and took off his hat and jacket and set them there.

"Since you're new in town, I'll work as your second between rounds."

"That won't be necessary," Teddy said.

Bat walked over.

"You ready to take me on?" he uttered in a low voice.

"As ready as I'll ever be. I guess we better make it look good for those who would like to see you dead."

Bat offered him a lopsided confident smile.

"I'll try my best to make it look real good, laddy."

Bat ducked between the ropes into the ring. He took off his shirt and handed it to brother Jim. Ed, who looked a lot more like Bat than Jim did, came over.

"He hits like a mule," Ed said. "Just so you know."

"I'll keep that in mind."

Everyone, including all three of the Masterson brothers, had confident smiles, like they shared a huge secret among themselves.

Teddy took off the shoulder-rig holster and handed it to Dog, who admired the lean tall frame of the detective. Dog held apart the ropes for Teddy to step into the ring.

The crowd surged forward and Teddy could hear bets being laid down, most all of them on Bat Masterson. A few bet on Teddy because the odds Dog was giving were ten to one in favor of Bat.

Bat walked over from his corner and said, "If I'm going to make this look legit, I'm going to hit hard. It won't be any disgrace if you get knocked down and stay down. Lots of men have."

"I guess I just won't let you hit me then."

Bat looked at him like he was waiting for the punch line of the joke.

"I guess that would be wisest, you not letting me hit you," he said.

Dog crawled through the ropes, said, "I'm going to referee, since my man here says he doesn't need a second."

"That's fine by me, if it's all right with him," Bat said.

Dog raised his voice for all the crowd to hear and signaled Jim to bang on a spittoon with the barrel of a pistol in lieu of a bell. "All bets down now, boys! The fight's about to begin . . ." and so on and so forth, announcing it as a long-held grudge between the two men stemming from some dispute years earlier on the Texas plains. It was a hell of a story, Teddy thought standing there listening to it. Finally Dog got on with it.

"You boys shake hands and come out fighting when Jim hits that spittoon again with his shooter," Dog said.

They shook hands and each walked back to their respective corner. Teddy could see there were slatterns in attendance, some of them smoking cigars. Several of them catcalled remarks about what a good-looking young man Teddy was. He tried ignoring such comments, choosing to concentrate on strategy for fighting Bat instead.

*Hell, let's get this over fast,* Teddy thought when Jim clanged the barrel of his shooter off the brass spittoon.

Bat came across the ring in short choppy steps, his fists held high. Teddy circled to Bat's right. Bat shot a left jab, but Teddy saw Bat telegraph it and ducked easily out of the way. The crowd roared. Teddy felt the rattlesnake in him take over. He moved smoothly, as though he were gliding on ice. Everything in his world grew silent and it looked like Bat was moving in slow motion. He shot a crunching left hook to Bat's lower ribs and when it landed, as he knew it would, he brought a right hand over the top of Bat's guard and caught him flush on the cheek.

The combination staggered the lawman and put a look of surprise on his face. Teddy gave him time to gather himself. He didn't want to embarrass the man too badly in front of his own townspeople.

Bat came rushing in and they ended up in a clinch along the ropes and some of the crowd pushed them back to the center of the ring. Dog stepped in to separate them. Bat pushed him away, threw a hard left-right combination to Teddy's body. But Teddy barely felt them in the state of mind he was in.

He threw his own combination: a flurry of six straight blows, all hitting their target and sending Bat to the floor.

Bat rose to one knee while Dog counted. A trickle of blood from over his right eye and two trickles from his nostrils looked like red ribbons. He struggled to his feet.

Teddy's and Bat's eyes met. Teddy could sense Masterson's doubt. Bat knew what he hadn't known before: that he was in against an irrepressible foe. But his own pride wouldn't allow him to quit.

He came at Teddy, who easily danced out of the way while delivering blow after blow—every punch like the strike of a snake to Bat's face and body, each doing a little more damage than the previous one. Bat swung wildly now in desperation, hoping to tag Teddy with a lucky punch. It was his only hope of redemption. It wasn't to be.

Teddy swayed out of the way of a roundhouse right and hit Bat with a solid left-right combination that dropped Bat to his knees just as the man struck the spittoon, indicating that the first round was over.

Jim and Ed helped Bat back to his corner. Teddy motioned Dog over and said, "This is foolish to go on. He has to know by now he can't win. Tell him to quit."

Dog went over and whispered in the ear of Bat what Teddy was advocating.

"Hell, I know I can't win," Bat said. "But I'm not quitting either. Tell him that." Bat spat a mouthful of blood.

"No use to go on, brother," Ed said.

"No use at all," Jim said.

"Yeah, no use at all. But let em carry me out, I ain't quitting."

Dog returned to Teddy's corner amid the hoorahs and cheering and curses of the crowd and told him what Bat had said.

"Then tell him I'll quit," Teddy said.

Dog shrugged and returned to Bat's corner and told him what Teddy was offering to do. The two combatants exchanged knowing looks. "The hell you will," Bat mouthed silently.

The spittoon was struck for round two and Bat came out, his movements slower now, more cautious, like an old man.

Teddy didn't want to brutalize the man. He needed to get it over quick. He feinted with his right and when Bat went for the fake Teddy caught him with a left hook that took him off his feet and landed him on the floor. Both of them and everyone in the house could see it was a blow Bat wouldn't get up from.

Dog began to count, reached ten, then waved his arms, shouting "It's all over."

There were a lot of groans while they revived Bat by splashing a bucket of ice water over him. Disappointed men paid the lucky few who'd bet on the lanky stranger.

"Tall man always beats a shorter one," someone said.

Teddy sat on a chair with both hands in a bucket of ice water. His hands hurt like hell. It had been a long time since he'd fought anyone like that. In a way it felt good, but in another way it felt terrible.

Dog brought him a whiskey with a beer chaser. "That was some piece of work you did in the ring," he said.

"How is Bat?"

"Oh, hell, he's coming around fine. He's a little glassy eyed still."

Teddy stood and walked over to where Bat was now sitting and took out a chair across from him, said loud enough for those still hanging out to hear, "I guess you'll damn well know who your betters are. Next time we cross paths it'll be more than just fists."

Bat was fingering one of his teeth, checking to see if it had been knocked loose. Bat looked at him with those dark troubling eyes. Saw none of the lingerers were within easy earshot.

"Thought you said you weren't a fighter?"

"I'm not, by nature. But I did box on my college boxing team."

Bat looked at his brothers, one eye swelling. "He boxed on his college team," he said. They nodded their heads. "I guess I owe you an apology."

"No, you don't owe me anything."

"I even hit you once?" Bat said.

"Yeah, I think a couple of times."

"I think from now on when it comes to boxing, I'll stick to refereeing. You didn't get hit, did you, Dog?"

Dog grinned. "No, but I lost my ass betting on you, Bat."

"Next time me and you fight, I'll bring my gun," Bat said loudly for the benefit of those along the bar. He said it with a crooked smile, his mouth full of wet red. "Whiskey," he said to brother Jim.

"We better do our meeting from now on in private," Teddy said, standing.

Bat sipped his whiskey, grimaced as the bite of it touched the split in his lip.

They each knew what respect was and how to give it and did, in that silent moment before Teddy walked over and shucked on his shoulder rig, then his coat and hat and went on out into the wild streets of Dodge again.

# *Chapter 9*

———◆———

Dirty Dave Rudabaugh said, "Boys, I'm tired of running from them Mastersons, ain't you? I'm tired of digging my way out of jails with spoons, ain't you?" The boys Dave was talking to simply looked at him and shook their heads.

"No, we ain't tired of running from the Mastersons," Cherokee Bill said. "Running from the Mastersons beats hell out of being shot and killed by 'em."

"It beats it all to hell seven ways," said Tom Tulip, Cherokee Bill's first cousin. There had been two others of Dave's group, but they'd long since fled, not waiting around for any more of Dirty Dave's outlaw plans.

"I'm thinking we ought to ride back to Dodge and just murder them sons a bitches, then we wouldn't have to run from 'em no more," Dirty Dave said.

"Go right ahead," Cherokee Bill said.

"Yeah, go right ahead, you got our permission," Tom Tulip said. Tom often repeated whatever Cherokee Bill said and added just a little of his own thinking on the end.

Dave looked at them with unveiled disgust.

"You boys is piss poor when it comes to partners. Why, you wouldn't even make carbuncles on a real partner's ass."

"Me and Tom is going down to the pistol barrel like we planned before the Mastersons caught us and put us in that mud jail," Cherokee Bill said. "You're welcome to come along."

"It's mean country, that pistol barrel is. They's a lot of low-down cutthroats hiding out in that country," Dave said. "You boys is liable for sure to get murdered by them that's worse'n us."

"Maybe so," Cherokee Bill said. "But they can't be no meaner down there than them Masterson brothers will be if they catch us again."

"Yeah, they can't be no meaner," Tom said. "Next time them Mastersons catch up to us they'll probably just shoot us and save themselves the trouble of having us escaping from 'em."

"Well, you boys at least ought to help me rob one more train before you go."

"What for? We dint get nothing off the last one but a bunch of mail and ain't a one of us can read," Cherokee Bill said.

"That's exactly why we ought to rob another train. This time we'll rob one that's got passengers on it. We'll take their wallets and pocket watches and we'll take the women's brooches and rings.

Why, we'll steal the gold fillings out of their teeth if we have to."

Tom Tulip looked at his cousin Cherokee Bill.

"You up for robbing any more trains and stealing gold fillings out of teeth?"

"Not me. I never did like the idea to rob a train on account of what happened to Jake Crowfoot that time."

"Me neither."

"Who's Jake Crowfoot?" Dave asked.

"He featured himself a first-rate train robber," Bill said. "He come out of Omaha. Wore two guns. Little feller. Real loud talker, always bragging what a magnificent train robber he was."

"Well, what happened to him?"

"He was trying to rob a Union and Pacific and fell under it. Cut him into tiny pieces. He was already little as it was."

"He was a lot littler when that train finished with him," Tom said. "He quit talking loud too."

Tom grinned at his joke and Cherokee Bill grinned at it too.

They both spit and then mounted their horses.

"We'll see you in Paris, France," Cherokee Bill said.

Dave watched them ride off. He didn't know what the hell Bill was talking about, saying they'd see him in Paris, France. And when the dust settled again, Dave told himself he was better off without the two of them and the other two, who'd ridden off soon as they broke out of jail.

"I'm better off," he said to the prairie wind.

But the thought of killing the Mastersons all by himself felt like a daunting task indeed. He'd have to find himself a new partner or three, and he thought he knew of just where he might find such—a place called Mister. He'd been to it once with his old gang—Buck Pierce and Hannibal Smith. They all three had hidden out there because it was a lawless little burg. Fact was, Buck and Hannibal might still be there. It cheered him like sunshine to think they could be. They were two mean bastards if there were ever mean bastards to be had. That was for sure. Mad-dog-killer mean. He'd just have to figure out something to get them to throw in with him and help him rub out the Mastersons. Of course, Buck and Hannibal could just as easily be dead as alive. They could have been hanged or shot by a posse. An outlaw's life was like love: never a sure bet and never for long.

He rode northeast, back in the general direction of Mister, which lay along Crooked Creek. It was just a shantytown.

He arrived about midnight. He saw that half the town had been burnt to the ground: that which lay on the west side of the main and only street. But the town on the east side of the street was still standing, three saloons and a dope den in total, untouched except by some smoke marks.

It did not take Dave long to locate Buck and Hannibal. They were busy beating a fellow senseless in front of one of the saloons, the word HOGSHEAD painted atop its false front.

Well, once Dave got a clearer look-see in the light cast by torches there in front of the saloon, he could see it was mostly Hannibal doing the beating and Buck doing the holding of the fellow getting beat. A whore in a yellow dress stood screaming like a banshee. Dave couldn't understand what she was screaming about, but it was clear that she wasn't happy with the situation. The beaten fellow looked like a rag doll being pummeled.

Dave sat his horse and watched with a certain admiration the handiwork of his old gang. Those boys were still mean bastards, judging by the way they were pulverizing the beat feller. Just the sort of partners Dave would need to go back to Dodge with and finish the Mastersons.

"Boys, let me buy you a drink to celebrate your victory over this no-account, I'm sure," Dave said when the two grew weary of beating the poor man and left him lying in the dirt. The whore in the yellow dress tried to comfort the felled man. His eyes were rolled back. It took the boys several seconds to recognize Dirty Dave because Hannibal was about blind drunk and Buck was too. They stood swaying like wheat in the wind.

"Why, we heard you was dead," Buck said when at last recognition penetrated his brain.

"Hanged by the Mastersons, we heard," Hannibal said.

"Up in Dodge," Buck said.

"Or somewhere," Hannibal said.

"As you can plainly see, I ain't dead hardly. And it will be a cold day in hell before I am, especially by the hand of them Mastersons."

Then Buck fell down, passed out cold, and Hannibal bent down to look at him and he fell down too. That's when the whore took her revenge and ran into a saloon and back out again with a spittoon and began banging the boys over the head with it until Dave pulled his Smith and Wesson revolver and said, "I'd sure hate to shoot a woman, especially one in such a pretty yellow dress, but thems' my old pards." Her battering had more or less aroused the boys to a lighter stupor.

"You boys is in need of a leader, I can see that," Dave said.

Dirty Dave managed to get them into the saloon, and once seated at a table and drinks ordered, he commenced to lay out his plan. But the boys passed out again before he could finish, so he drank himself into a stupor as well, and awoke lying on a pool table with the morning sun striped across his face. The boys were asleep on the floor like big dogs.

Dave spilled a bucket of beer on them and they awoke growling.

"Goddamn, I can see this ain't gone be easy," Dave said.

Dave told them the big fat lie he'd concocted about an easy bank in Dodge they could rob.

"Probably's got twenty, thirty thousand dollars in gold sitting in it just waiting for a couple of mean fuckers like us to come and take it out," Dave said.

"What about them Mastersons?" Buck said, rubbing his eyes to get the sting of beer and sleep out.

"Yeah, I heard they was the law up around in there," Hannibal said. His breath stank like coal oil.

"That's the beauty of my plan," Dave said.

"What is?" Buck said.

"Beauty?" Hannibal said.

"We sneak in and kill them Mastersons in their sleep and then rob the bank. Rather than rob the bank and have 'em chase us, we rub out the law first and then they ain't nobody to chase us. She's a beaut ain't she, boys, my plan?"

"Bank robbing, huh?" Buck said, rubbing his jaw.

"That's a clever notion," Hannibal said.

"You know where I got the idea?" Dave said.

The boys shook their heads.

"The James brothers down in Missouri. They's the first ones to rob a bank. They got it down to perfection too. I reckoned they robbed a hundred banks by now and made themselves at least a million dollars in easy loot. I reckon soon every outlaw in the country will be taking up the trade. We sure enough ought to get in on it ourselves before all the banks get robbed."

"Is that how they do it, them Jamses? Kill the law first then rob the banks?" Buck said.

"No, that idea is an original, something I thought up personal."

Hannibal was quiet for a long time. Then he slapped a hand down hard on the table and said, "I got me an idea too."

"What is it?" Buck said.

"Let's kill them damn Mastersons and rob *all* the banks in Dodge!"

"Say, that's a sparkling idea," Buck said.

"It sure is," Dirty Dave said. "We best get started right away."

"Can't," Hannibal said.

"Why not?"

"Buck's getting married in a few days."

"Married?"

"Well, if she ain't changed her mind," Buck said. "She was mighty upset about me and Hannibal beating the hell out of her daddy."

"You mean that whore in the yellow dress?" Buck looked at Dave with flinty eyes.

"Careful what you say, that's my sweetheart you're talking about."

"Why'd you beat him if he was your sweetheart's daddy?" More silence. Dave and Buck and Hannibal trading looks back and forth.

"I can't remember," Buck said.

"I can't either," Hannibal said. "We was all just drinking and having a good time and next I know, we was out there on the street fighting."

"Yeah," Buck said. "You know how we get when we get drunk and to fighting. We're like a pair of wildcats, Hannibal and me . . ."

"Like wildcats," Hannibal affirmed.

"Well boys, all I can say is all that gold might not be too long in that bank. Some other mean fuckers like us could get the idea to rob it too, you know, and beat us to the punch."

"It'll have to wait," Buck said. "I ain't never been married before, but I have been an outlaw many times over. And Hannibal here is to be my best man. I guess if you can't wait until after Saturday, you'll have to go rob that bank by your lonesome."

"Well, I reckon a few days won't matter all that much. I doubt any other outlaws will come up with my same plan. Most of 'em ain't all that smart."

"I thought you was a train robber by trade," Buck said.

"Was, ain't no more, not since what happened to Jake Crowfoot."

"Who's Jake Crowfoot and what happened to him?"

So Dirty Dave ordered them all a round of drinks and told them the story of Jake Crowfoot falling under the Union Pacific train—embellishing it somewhat since he never actually knew Jake Crowfoot or the exact circumstances of his life and tragic death—and pausing just long enough to deliver the punch line about how much littler

Jake became and how he wasn't a loud talker no
more.

The boys laughed like hell.

And Dirty Dave did too.

# Chapter 10

———————————•———————————

Teddy stopped by the Wright House after leaving the Lone Star. He wanted to see Mae, to explain he wasn't like all the other men, the ones she'd referred to with her last comment. But as he got closer, he realized that maybe he was like all the other men, like every man who ever lived. He had too much pride even to suit himself. He felt badly about having beaten Bat in the ring in front of the people who knew and trusted him as their county sheriff. He should have turned down the challenge, told Bat to go to hell and go it alone and gotten on a train and gone back to Chicago, where he probably really belonged.

He paused in front of the Wright House. What was the point of his going in and trying to convince Mae of something he wasn't?

To hell with it.

He walked on to his hotel, and went up to his room.

The more he thought about it, the more he was convinced he should leave. He began packing his valise.

What had coming to the West gained him, really? A few years of being a cowboy. And now he was a wanted man, and doing work he wasn't even sure he was qualified to do. He packed his shirts. Socks. Then he found the silver flask he'd put in the drawer with his spare clothes. The flask Cody had given him out of gratitude. He stroked it with his hand, his knuckles scraped and swollen from the fight.

COL. WFC was etched into the side of the flask. He unscrewed the cap and took a pull of Cody's best liquor, and all it did was remind him of Anne and death there along the Dismal River.

He took another pull, draining the last of it, then screwed the cap back on and tossed it into the valise along with his shirts and socks. Came a knock at the door.

He opened it. Mae was standing there.

Neither of them said anything for a moment.

"You win your fistfight?" she said.

He nodded, stepped aside so she could enter the room.

He watched her as she looked around, saw that she saw the open valise there on the bed.

"Leaving, huh?"

"Yeah," he said.

"You get into a fistfight and leave town. You sound like a cowboy," she said.

"I was a cowboy at one time. Maybe some of it's carried over."

"I doubt that."

"Why do you doubt it?"

"I've been around enough to know a thing or two."

"Meaning?"

"Meaning I know you're not just some cowboy who drifted into town. Meaning I think you're a lot more than what you represent yourself as. You like others to think there's not much to you, but I think there is."

"Well, maybe you don't know as much about me as you think you do."

She cast her gaze toward his hands. Shook her head.

"Was it worth it, the fight?"

"I thought it was necessary at the time."

"Jesus, you're such a fool," she said, and came and put her arms around him and kissed him.

It was a kiss of sanctuary. A place he could retreat into for a long full moment.

She pulled back, looked at him.

"This is what you wanted, right?" she said.

"I don't know."

"Maybe you need to think about it some more," she said, kissing him again.

He tried hard not to let thoughts of Anne or Kathleen creep in, found it impossible to keep them out, then became completely lost in Mae's passion for him. Everything seemed to turn and turn there in the room as they embraced, as though the world was circling around them. She sighed when he returned her kisses.

"It's been a long time for me," she whispered.

He guided her to the bed.

"You're leaving . . ." she said as he began to unbutton her dress, she his shirt.

He kissed her into silence, felt the fluttering of her heart as he laid his hand gently on her breast. She drew him closer to her.

"You're leaving . . ." she repeated.

He kissed the words from her lips.

And later they lay together beneath the blankets, she in the crook of his arm, her head resting on his shoulder, her body melded to his as though they'd become one person sharing the same heart, the same flesh and blood.

They lay like that a long, long time. Light retreated from the room and it grew dark and he said, "Do you want me to light the lamp?"

"No," she said. "Don't move."

He felt her hands tracing over his body, as though she were a blind child exploring an unfamiliar landscape. The scent of her hair was a memory of the summers he'd spent as a boy, that distant flowery scent that always seemed to be in the air where gardens grew.

"There are so many things I want to tell you," she said.

"Go ahead and tell me."

"No."

"Why not?"

"Because you're leaving."

He wasn't sure if he was leaving now or not.

She kissed the sore knuckles of his hand and her lips were like butterflies touching them.

"I feel sometimes like I don't belong anywhere," he said. "I guess that's why I'm always ready to leave one place for another."

"I feel that way too."

"Tell me one thing about you I don't know," he said.

"Not right now."

"If not now, when?"

"Soon," she said.

She kissed him and her kiss felt like resurrection. Time took wing as their passions again consumed them.

Sometime during the night they must have fallen asleep.

Their sleeping was disturbed by another knock at the door. Instinctively Teddy reached for his pistol as Mae stirred half awake next to him.

"What is it?" she muttered as he climbed from the bed.

"Nothing," he said, pulling on his trousers. "Stay put."

He opened the door just far enough to see Frenchy LeBreck standing there, dark and fidgeting.

"What do you want?"

"I came to see you about that work you said you sometimes do." Frenchy tried looking past Teddy into the room but Teddy blocked his view.

"I'll come see you," Teddy said.

"We could discuss it right now."

"No, now's not a good time."

"You've got someone with you, is that it?"

"Name a time at your place," Teddy said.

"Tomorrow, anytime after noon or so."

"Fine."

Teddy closed the door and went back to the bed.

"Who was that?" Mae said.

"Man who wants to offer me a job."

"I thought you were leaving Dodge . . ."

"Maybe not."

"Because someone offered you a job?"

Teddy slipped into the bed beside her.

"No, not because of a job," he said.

She gathered herself against him and he didn't mind it that she did. Her skin felt warm and smooth, an invitation.

"Listen," she said. "I don't want you to change your plans on account of me, us, what happened here tonight."

"Shhh . . ." he said.

Her mouth and flesh were soft and warm as a south Texas night and he felt at ease with her there, next to him, beneath him. And when the first morning light flowed into the room, he found she'd gone and he wasn't sure if he'd dreamt her visit or if she'd really been there with him.

He closed his eyes, telling himself it hadn't been a dream and, as he did, he remembered other loves, other places, and other times.

# *Chapter 11*

———•◦•———

To John Sears, it seemed like time passed a lot slower since Teddy had gone north again. John was by his very nature a loner, but he'd come to rely on the younger man for companionship, someone to drink with and talk to, and most important, someone to trust.

Everything seemed a little less promising without Teddy around. He owed the younger man much for saving his life back up in New Mexico. It was as close as he'd ever come to dying, and the worst part about it wasn't the dying but the knowing when it would happen.

He thought about the woman he'd shot, dreamt about her, and the dreams were always sad. He'd done a lot of hard things in his life, but shooting the woman had been the worst, in his book, even if it was more or less accidental.

Sometimes the priest came and sat with him and drank and talked about the old times.

John would ask the priest what he was before he'd become a priest and the priest said, "I was a sailor, John."

"You miss it?"

"Sometimes I do."

It struck John that the priest never got drunk no matter how much tequila he drank, and John tried hard not to get drunk either, but sometimes he couldn't help it.

"How'd you lose your thumb, John?" the priest asked him one time when they were drinking in the shade of a jacale.

"Gunfight," John said, looking at the nub of flesh.

"Did you do much of that, fight with guns?"

"When I was younger I run with a pretty bad crowd, Padre."

"I suppose it's hard to handle a gun without your thumb," the priest said.

"It puts a crimp in your style."

The priest smiled, the evening sun glowing in his weathered face. John could imagine him on the foredeck of a ship, the wind in his face.

"What made you want to become a priest?"

"I had an empty place inside of me, John. It's a thing that's hard to explain. I tried every which way to fill it, but nothing did. Then one bad night it came to me what I needed to do to fill that place."

John said, "I think I know what you mean."

The priest looked at him as he took up the olla of tequila and sipped from it and then handed it over to John.

"I guess I always knew you did since that time

you made your confession about shooting the woman," the priest said.

The boy Chico came down the street with his donkey. They both looked dusty and tired and the priest called the boy over and spoke to him in Spanish, and John knew enough to understand the priest had invited him to come to supper, had told him to go wash himself and put on a fresh shirt and come to the little hacienda where he and the woman stayed and to tell her that the priest had invited him to supper.

The boy smiled and John could see there was a certain sad pride in the boy's dark eyes, as though he knew the truth about the priest being his father but knew also he had no right to mention it or make claim to such a thing.

"*Gracias*," the boy said and led off tugging the rope tied to the donkey's halter.

"He's a good boy, that one," the priest said.

"What happened to his folks?" John asked.

The priest didn't answer John's question but instead sipped some more of the tequila and said, "I better get on back and help Selena with supper."

And John once more felt alone as the brown sky grew darker now that the sun was setting off to the west.

It wasn't long after Teddy had gone north again that the woman began coming around. At first John just thought she was being pleasant, bringing him freshly made tortillas and sometimes fruit.

She seemed shy, curious as a cat, moved like a cat, quiet and stealthy, her eyes ever watchful of him.

Even though she was a mute, John liked talking to her.

"These folks around here give you much grief over being the priest's woman?" John asked one time after he felt like he had gotten to know her well enough. But soon as he asked the question he was sorry he had. It wasn't any of his business.

"Hell, I guess I shouldn't be asking such things," he said apologetically.

She shook her head no. He wasn't sure if she was saying no, the folks in the village didn't give her any grief, or if she was saying no, it was okay for him to ask her.

"He's a good man, the priest is," John said.

She nodded.

John wondered what it was that brought her around so often to visit him. He chalked most of it up to simple curiosity, but one day he said, "He ever mind you come and visit me?"

She hesitated a moment then shook her head no.

"No, I guess there's no reason he would. He knows I'd never try nothing with you."

John saw something flash through her eyes.

"I just mean it's not that you're not an attractive woman or anything, Selena—you are. I just meant to say the priest knows how much I respect him and out of that respect I wouldn't . . ."

John didn't know how to explain it right.

After that day Selena didn't come around for nearly a week and it troubled him that she didn't and he didn't know quite what he should do if anything. Thing was, he missed her visits and he wasn't sure in his own mind that he should even feel that much toward her.

Then when she did return finally, bringing him some shirts he'd paid her to mend and wash, he felt glad to see her. He made her some tea and they sat and drank it and John said, "I'm gonna just sort of keep my mouth shut from now on, for every time I open it, I stick my boot in."

The way the light fell through the window that day, the way it fell on her black silken hair and across the side of her face made John realize how pretty she was and he had to look away not to stare.

And later after she left and he went to put his mended shirts on a shelf he found the little note tucked in between them.

It read: *He doesn't mind. I want to be your friend.*

John sat down on the edge of the cot and read the words a thousand times, trying to decipher the full meaning behind them.

He told himself nearly as many times the note was innocent. How could it be otherwise?

The boy watched the woman coming and going from the priest's hacienda and each time it troubled him.

# Chapter 12

———◆———

The Rose had come to Frenchy LeBreck that night seeking mercy, seeking refuge. He took one look at her and gasped, even as hard a man as he was and even having seen a thousand terrible things in his life.

"Come in," he said and meant it.

She sobbed when she tried to tell him of the brutality laid on her by the hands of Bone Butcher.

"Shhh, shhh," he said. "Have a drink," and poured her some cognac, for it was better for the spirit than the harsh frontier liquor most out in this rough country sought succor from.

She took to it like medicine that could cure the bruises and more, the deeper hurt. She took to it like it was a salve and mother's milk, which she had not had since she was a child.

"Isn't that better?" he said after a time of watching her.

"Yes, better," she said.

"Why come to me?" he asked when at last the sobs stopped lurching through her and she stopped shivering like a frightened kitten. He had lit a single lamp and its light fell on her in a soft saffron glow that helped disguise the more obvious bruises.

"I heard you was kinder than most," she said.

He wanted to laugh, to ask her who would say such a thing when the general consensus was he was like all the others, out to make a dollar any way he could in a town that swallowed whole the beguiled and foolish and would pick clean the pockets of any unsuspecting soul with a bit of loose change. He had no compunction to do otherwise. It was, after all, a world in which one either survived or did not.

"Oh, I don't guess you heard right about me," he said. "I'm no different than any of the others."

She looked at him, one eye swelling darkly colored as a plum.

"If I go back now, he will only beat me worse. He suspects I've cheated him in every way a woman can cheat a man, this in the face of what I do for him, what I do to survive . . ."

He put a hand upon her shoulder and she leaned toward him like a slender willow bending toward a flowing creek and reached for him with tender arms that were like limbs reaching for the sun. He understood her need to survive and admired it. He wasn't sure what to do, but knew what he'd like to do, knew what he'd always thought about doing whenever he saw her, even knowing that she was the property of one Bone Butcher, a murderously jealous man. He oft thought of her as a flower owned by a man who had no appreciation for flowers but who kept her in spite of his lack of understanding and appreciation.

"I can put you up for the night," he said.

She kissed the hand he'd laid upon her shoulder and held it tightly in her own as though she would never release it.

He did not mind. He allowed it to be held and felt the warm fine bones of her hand as some sort of comfort against all the black days and nights he'd lived since leaving Louisiana and before there the South of France, vowing even as he left those places that he would return someday. The West was a ragged and wooly place without a single drop of culture, but a place too where a man who was shrewd enough could make a small fortune from the misfortune of others.

"Would you like more cognac?" he asked.

"Yes," she said demurely; all of the harsh realities of who she was and what she had been and who it was who claimed her gone now out of her, drained away in that tender moment. To Frenchy LeBreck, the Rose of Cimarron was a pure flower.

He poured them each a glass and sat there beside her on the horsehair divan not inches away and watched her put the glass to her lips, to that tender mouth that seemed to him in the low light of the lamp hardly stained at all by the mouths of a thousand men, Bone Butcher's included, and he wanted to kiss that mouth himself but refrained.

"Does he do this to you often?"

"More lately than ever before."

"Why do you allow it?"

She gave way to more tears when he asked this of her.

"I'm sorry," he said. "It's none of my business."

"What choice is there for a woman like me in such a place if not to whore and drink with men and be their good-luck charm as they gamble and later their comfort up in a room they pay for by the hour? I made the foolish mistake of becoming one man's whore and not for the multitude. I would have been better off staying what I was than what I've become."

"Oh, I don't need to know everything," he said.

"But you do know everything," she said. "Your business is the same as his."

"No, not the same, not exactly. I don't beat my girls . . ." And instantly he was sorry he had said it just that way, for he saw how she flinched as if his words were like fists about to strike her again.

"I'm sorry," he said. "I didn't mean to . . ."

She sighed and leaned against him, nearly spilling the last drops of cognac from her glass.

"Oh, I'd kill him if only I could. I'll kill him and run away if only I had some place to run to."

It made him think.

The weight of her against him like that was the first such weight he'd felt in a very long time. For he did not consort with whores, knowing as he did the diseases they were prone to, the cruel and harsh ways they tended to laugh at anything they did not respect, how they talked among themselves about the inadequacies of the men who visited them. These things, along with the Catholicism that had scarred him, it seemed, with too much guilt, thinking as he did that Jesus was always watching to see and judge his every move. Still, the guilt hadn't stopped him from pursing the pleasure trade, for he saw it as nearly honorable as many other types of work and more than some. And the work paid far better, him knowing, as a man, that men would always have a need and a willingness to pay for their pleasure. The farther from civilization he plied his trade, the better. And if he had to get down on his knees and pray every night for forgiveness from his sins, by God, he would and did. Sometimes when he drank too much and his mood turned gregarious he told himself a private joke about how his knees had calluses from so much praying.

She didn't seem a sin to him as she leaned against him breathing easily now, wiping away the last of the tears as she sipped more cognac. She seemed to him not what she was, but more a virgin. She seemed a woman who had at least temporarily emancipated herself from her cruel master. And for this small bravery alone he admired her.

*I would kill him if only I could.* The words resonated in his heart like the steady beating of a drum.

He put his arm around her tentatively and she did not resist or draw away but gave over to him more of herself, coming so close he could smell the smoke of men's cigars in her hair amid her other scents of perfume and fear.

It raked his very skin, the scent of her.

"What should I do?" she said at last.

"Stay here with me," he said, without giving the least thought to the consequences of what all that would mean come the next day or the next or the next.

Bone Butcher often publicly swore the vengeance he'd take on any man who fooled with her. But in that moment Frenchy did not consider such threats, for the night was black and the doors to his place now locked and a loaded gun was handy enough if he needed one. Her weight against him there on the divan gave him strength to consider any possibility.

For once, he felt like a man who knew the price other men willingly paid for love and would pay again if asked to do it. He wanted to say how he would liberate her but was afraid he might frighten her even more.

His eyes strayed into the shadowy recesses of the room and he thought—wondered—if Jesus was watching him now, judging him, adding to his book of transgressions.

"I know just the thing," he said. "Wait here . . ."

And he went into an anteroom and heated water, pail after pail of it, and filled the copper tub he kept as one luxury he refused to do without. His girls often used it and he quite approved their penchant for doing so. And when he'd filled it full, he came and retrieved her and said, "For you," and pointed toward the steaming bath.

"Oh," she said, with genuine surprise and delight.

He turned away thinking she would want to undress in private.

"I don't mind if you want to see me," she said.

"No, no," he said. "Let this be a thing only for you."

She kissed him tenderly on the mouth and he felt like the flame the moth was drawn to, the tip of the flame hot inside him, a dancing hot tongue to ward off the darkness that had been there for so many years.

He turned and said as he did, "I'll be back soon." Then went in search of the man who'd visited his saloon the other night, the tall young man who had pulled his coat open wide enough to reveal a hanging pistol and said "I do certain kinds of work" and gave his name before departing.

So he knocked on the door and the young man answered and though he was unwilling to conduct any sort of business at that hour did agree to come again the next day to the saloon and discuss it, and it was all he could do and it was enough.

When he returned he found her just lifting herself from the copper tub, the water sheeting off her pearl white body where he could see, here and there aside from her beauty, the dark bruises put there by Bone Butcher, whose roughness knew no limits.

She did not try and hide herself from his eyes but instead turned fully so he could see her, her arms hanging loose at her sides.

"Am I beautiful to you, Frenchy?"

"Yes," he admitted.

She stepped from the tub as he reached for a towel, and came toward him like that, wet and beautiful and bruised in places that in that moment seemed not to mar her beauty at all, and stepped into the towel he held for her. Then he wrapped it about her like a cloak and she stood trembling.

"I'm going to fix it," he said.

"Fix what?"

"The troubles you're having with Bone."

Her eyes appealed to him. "He's a very dangerous man," she said.

"I know, but dangers can come in many forms."

"I like the way your voice is, your little accent."

"I think there was a reason you came to me and not someone else," he said.

"Reason knows no reason," she said.

She led him by the hand up to the little loft where he slept above the room where the tub stood, the water in it cooling now as though saddened by her departure. He looked at it just before disappearing into the loft with her and thought how he would have liked it very much to have taken a cloth and gently washed from her the bruises and scars placed there.

She dropped the towel and showed him where to touch her.

"This isn't necessary," he said.

She pouted.

He realized how much older than she he was. It did not seem to matter when she went and lay upon the cot, the dim light from below having climbed the stair as well and trying desperately to give the room some hope. And upon the bed she reclined, cast in shadow and that little bit of light, which caused a stirring of his passion for her and made him resolve to do whatever it would take to liberate her from the terrible force that deemed it necessary to bruise her and damage her.

"Come lay with me, Frenchy."

He knew he could not, would not resist her invitation.

Taking off his clothes he felt the eyes of Jesus as well as her own on him. He heard chants in Latin, smelled the burning incense, saw the great Gothic spires of Notre Dame rising against the doughy gray skies of Paris.

She gathered him in like a young girl gathering in a sheaf of wheat and held him to her and kissed his unshaved cheeks, his knife-sharp nose, his eyelids now closed over his dark eyes.

"I wish it were you who owned me and not Bone Butcher," she said, her voice a feathery whisper of hope.

He wished the same, but owning seemed too harsh a term for it.

"I would give anything if I belonged to you instead of him."

The little light that had crawled up the stair with them wavered in the room against one wall, then expired as the lamp that had borne it drank the last of the oil in its glass bottom and guttered out. Then they were there in the dark, held together like that, two near strangers until this moment, both desperate for things to be other than what they were.

Frenchy had a plan, he thought a good one, and told himself that he would tell her about it someday, but for now he was content to lie there in her arms and let her cling to him and he to her and let the rest of the night do what it would.

# Chapter 13

When Teddy awoke the second time, the bed was empty of her and he knew it hadn't been a dream. He'd slept soundly and hadn't heard her leave. He worried that she'd awakened and regretted their night shared. He quickly dressed and that's when he found the note there atop the bureau leaning against the packed valise.

*If you leave, I will miss you. If you stay, come by and see me at work. Affectionately,*

*Mae.*

He felt the thinnest thread of relief. He realized too that he was as starved as a wolf.

On his way to the Wright House he stopped off at the telegrapher's to check for any messages from George Bangs. There was one. He took it outside and read it in the sunlight. The weather was uncommonly good, the winds warm, no sign of storms or other trouble.

*Have you uncovered anything? Inform me of
any progress. No further developments on
Las Vegas situation. Have contact with the
circuit judge, old friend of Allan's, good
where you're concerned but not likely for
Mr. Sears. Tracking information on Carnahan's relative. Awaiting word from you.*

*George Bangs Esq.*

He wondered as he crossed the street exactly
what information George might have uncovered
concerning the female relative of Horace's killer.
He dodged a wagon pulled by a four-horse team
and a cursing teamster and entered the Wright
House. Mae was waiting on a table of ladies wearing large hats. She saw him and came over and
stood there looking down at him where he sat.

"Why'd you leave without saying a proper
good-bye?" he asked.

"I was already a bit late for work as it was," she
said. "Besides, I wasn't sure if you'd feel differ-
ently toward me, us—what happened . . ."

"No, I don't feel any different toward you . . .
at least not in a negative way. It almost felt like a
dream to me."

"It wasn't a dream, Teddy."

He heard a church bell ringing and realized it
was Sunday.

"What time do you get off work?"

"Not until five o'clock."

"Can I stop by so we can go for a walk?"

"If that's your pleasure."

"It is."

"Do you want to order breakfast?"

"I already see what I want."

Color rose in her cheeks. He ordered coffee, scrambled eggs, ham, biscuits, butter, and molasses.

"Whatever could have made you so ravenous, Mr. Blue?" she teased, then walked off toward the kitchen before he could answer. He realized he liked her. He liked her a lot, for having barely known her for no more than a few days. She was that kind of woman: easy to get to know, easier still to like.

Dog Kelly came in wearing a cellulose collar that looked tight around his throat, and sporting his familiar swallowtail coat now looking like he'd at least spanked most of the dust out of it. He had on a new beaver hat. He came over immediately and sat down across from Teddy.

"You finished eating, or just waiting to get started?"

"Waiting to start."

"Good. You don't mind, I'll eat with you." Dog's eyes were their usual bloodshot red.

"You ever sleep?" Teddy asked.

"Not if I can help it. Here and there some. Catnaps mostly. About all I can stand is taking catnaps."

Mae brought the coffeepot and two cups.

"Morning Mae," Dog said.

"Morning Mayor."

Dog's smile was like a storm-weathered fence of brown crooked stakes. Mae poured coffee into their cups and asked Dog if he wanted his usual— flapjacks and bacon—and he nodded appreciatively and watched Mae's backside as she went off.

"Nice woman, that Mae," Dog said.

Teddy didn't reply.

"I think maybe I know who it is wants the Masterson boys rubbed out," Dog said, spooning sugar into his coffee and keeping his voice low.

"Who?"

"Angus Bush is who I'm betting."

"Why him?"

"A feller who used to work for him tending bar came into my place last night drunk as a turkey and was grumbling how the Mastersons was siphoning off lots of Angus's trade by serving better liquor and hiring all the best-looking whores. Feller said Angus had to lay him off because business was down."

"That's pretty thin evidence."

"I know it is, but hell, it's at least something to think about, wouldn't you say?"

"I had a visitor last night—Frenchy LeBreck. He wants to offer me a job."

"Doing what?"

"I'll find out when I go see him this afternoon, but my guess is it's to kill somebody. You always put that much sugar in your coffee?"

Dog looked at the fourth spoonful he was dropping into his cup.

"Helps keep me awake. You think it's the Mastersons he wants you to kill?"

Teddy shrugged, said, "I'll find out this afternoon."

Mae brought them their breakfasts and looked Teddy directly in the eyes and said, "Is there anything else you'd like?" Teddy hoped Dog was too concentrated on his flapjacks to have noticed the bold flirtation. Dog was already digging into them.

"No ma'am, not this minute. Perhaps later."

"I'll check back on you boys," she said and went off to the table with the ladies in the large hats.

Dog ate like a wanted man with the posse pulling up outside.

"You even taste those?" Teddy asked when Dog had stuffed the last bit of flapjack into his mouth and swallowed it practically without chewing it.

"Mmmm, they's good," Dog said. Droplets of molasses clung to his chin. "Gotta go, church is starting. You let me know what you find out with Frenchy and I'll sniff around more on Angus. We gone put the bad brothers under the sod."

Mae came over after Dog left.

"Was it Dog Kelly who came and knocked on your door last night to offer you a job?" she said.

"No."

"You going to tell me more about that?"

"Probably, but not now, not here."

"So I can expect you to come by when I get off today?"

"I'm counting on it."

"I could pack us a meal and we could ride out on the prairies and have a picnic, even though it's not exactly the season for picnics."

"That sounds like a fine idea. I'll see about renting us a cab."

She smiled and he did too.

He went down to the stables and made arrangements to rent a cab, then went over to the barbershop and sat his turn waiting for a shave. A barbershop was a good place to hear gossip.

"I'm surprised so many places are open on a Sunday," he said to the barber when he climbed into his chair.

"Only the rich can afford to take a day off," the barber said. "You want the works?"

"Just a shave."

"You ain't no cowboy."

"How can you tell?"

"You ain't got no cowboy haircut."

"Bowl around the head?"

"That's right. They come in here off the trail all butchered-looking from getting their hair cut by their pards with sheep shears and expect me to make 'em look pretty. I tell em I ain't no miracle worker, and 'sides, whores don't care what you look like and neither does a barkeep. Long as you got money in your pockets you could look like a gol-dang dog."

The man snapped out a barber's cape and snugged it around Teddy's neck, then wrapped his face in a hot damp towel. Teddy could hear him stropping his razor, brushing up the lather in the soap mug.

The barber talked about the weather and religion and politics and his sick wife and dumb kids and about everything that came to his thoughts, and for once Teddy didn't mind hearing about another man's troubles; it made his own pale in comparison. To think about having to cut hair and give shaves every day for a living was unsettling. He thought about men like John Sears, who wouldn't do any sort of work except what could be done from on the back of a horse, men who'd rather be dead and in the ground than tied to a regular job for regular pay.

He closed his eyes and heard only the *snick, snick* of the scissors and it was a comforting sound to him. When the barber finished his cutting, he daubed warm lather on Teddy's cheeks and deftly scraped off the growth of days-old whiskers.

"Here," the barber said and handed Teddy a bottle of bay rum. "Make you smell like a New York dandy."

"Why not?"

Then the barber said, "I notice you carry your piece in a shoulder rig. Unusual. Only man I ever knew to do that was a lawman in Philadelphia. He was real good with it."

Teddy pulled on his coat, said, "I just always thought of it as discretionary, that's all."

"Discretionary, huh?"

"How much do I owe you?"

"Two bits."

Teddy dropped the coins into the man's palm.

"You staying in town long?"

"For a time."

"Come on back when you need another shave or a haircut."

"I'll do that."

"Hope I didn't talk your ears off."

Teddy fingered his cheeks and chin then settled the Stetson on his head.

"You didn't."

Jim Masterson entered the shop just as Teddy was ready to leave. The two men exchanged glances, Jim saying, "Hidy" and Teddy returning the greeting. The barber said, "Come sit in this chair and let me shore you of them long locks," and Jim settled in as Teddy went out the door. A cool wind blew down the street. It was a good morning thus far, Teddy thought.

# *Chapter 14*

———◆———

Bat was daydreaming of high-caliber places like Philadelphia and Boston and New York City when Ed came into the Lone Star and said, "I could use your help."

"What is it?"

"Mattie Silks shot her pimp and is threatening to kill Bucktooth Nell."

"Lovers' spat, I take it," Bat said with a half grin.

"Goddamn, this is serious, Bat."

"Where's your deputies?"

"One's out sick with the gout and O'Dell is off hunting antelope."

Bat straightened from where he'd been leaning on the bar sipping a cocktail as he daydreamed.

"Where's Mattie at now?"

"Up in Nell's crib. She's cussing and saying how she's going to blow Nell's brains out."

"Over Beaver Jack?"

"Who else?"

"Pimps and whores," Bat said disgustedly.

They strode down the street to the Long

Branch and looked dangerous doing it. A sizeable crowd had gathered in the saloon and stood looking up toward the second floor, where the cribs were located.

Dog Kelly was among the spectators. "Boys, we got a situation on our hands. It ain't good business having whores shooting pimps and other whores. Pimps is okay, but whores is precious . . ."

"Just say the word," Ed said, "and we'll burn everything south of these tracks to the ground."

"We was to do that, the cowboys would burn up the north half next time they bring a herd in," Dog said glumly. "One hand always washes the other."

They could hear Nell's shrieks and Mattie's cussing her, saying such as, "You damn backstabbing trollop!"

"How'd this start?" Bat said.

Dog Kelly seemed to have the story as well as anyone.

"Mattie caught Beaver Jack rutting with Nell, or the other way around. Shot him twice, once in the liver, the other through the arm. He's in a bad way far as I can tell when they carried him out of here. Now she aims to kill Nell for trying to steal her man."

"What's stopping her?" Ed asked.

"I don't know, I guess she wants to put the fear of Jesus in Nell first, let her squirm a little before she plugs her."

"Women," Bat said, and started up the stairs taking them two at a time, Ed on his heels.

"Mattie," Bat called through the door.

"What?"

"It's Bat Masterson. Ed's out here too. Why don't you let Nell come on out and stop all this foolishness?"

"She'll come out toes up, the way I found her underneath Jack."

"Don't be talking nonsense now, girl."

"You seen Beaver?"

"No, he's been carried over to Doc's, the way I understand it."

"Is he dead?"

Bat looked at Ed, Ed shrugged.

"No, he isn't dead. Just shot a little, nothing too serious. I'm sure he'll forgive you once he heals."

"Oh Jesus!" Mattie's cry was full of remorse, it sounded like. "Jesus I dint mean to kill him!"

"You didn't kill him," Ed repeated.

"We'll just chalk this whole thing up to a lovers' spat," Ed said. "But you have to let Nell go."

"I aim to kill this damn strumpet."

"That'd get you hanged, Nell. You know I'd hate like hell to have to hang a woman, but a lot of these folks would see it as a pure spectacle, something to do during the slow time of the year. You wouldn't want to become a spectacle, would you?"

"I don't care!"

Dog had climbed the stairs as well and now stood next to Ed, impressed yet again by Bat's use of two-bit words. *Spectacle!* He liked it.

"Mattie, you'd be the biggest dang spectacle this town was ever to see if we have to hang you. You'd be a bigger spectacle than the time Wild Bill's wife brought her circus to town. More folks'd come to see you get hanged than what went to see them elephants." Dog felt proud of his ability to employ the word spectacle in his argument.

"Is that you, Dog?"

"Sure is. Bat's right, you oughter listen to him."

For a long time nobody said anything.

"Shit, Mattie, I've got things to do," Bat said. "I'm coming in. If you're so damn intent on taking life, take mine." And with that Bat kicked open the door.

Mattie stood with both hands holding a big Navy Colt, its barrel pointed the general direction of Bucktooth Nell who was cowering on a loveseat covered in red damask.

Bat reached out and took hold of the revolver, the web of his hand falling between hammer and cylinder to prevent an accidental shooting.

"Turn it loose Mattie, nice and easy," Bat ordered.

Mattie had venom in her eyes for Nell.

"It takes two to tangle," Dog Kelly said. "Remember that, Mattie; it ain't Nell's fault entirely. It's some of Beaver Jack's too."

"You shot Beaver twice, I guess you could count one of them bullets was for Nell here," Ed said. "Seems about even up to me, don't it you?"

"You want us to arrest you, Mattie, or would you rather just go on back to your room and get your things packed and catch the next stage out?" Bat asked.

Mattie stood there trembling, the defeated temptress, her shoulders slumped, knowing she'd lost at the game of love the way some lost at cards or roulette.

"Can I stop over to Doc's and see Beaver first?"

"Sure," Ed said. "Long as you ain't armed."

They escorted her down the stairs and out the front doors. Nell stayed in her room, shaking like an aspen in an autumn wind, big fat tears rolling down her cheeks.

Once the crowd saw the show was over, they went back to their homes and businesses, and some ordered a drink and some felt cheated because they'd arrived too late to see the first shooting, to see Beaver Jack carried out. All they saw were the drops of blood the swamper was mopping up—not much in the way of excitement.

Ed walked Mattie over to Doc's, where he watched her weep and kiss the much-in-agony Beaver Jack upon his lips, saying as she did, "I loved you hard, you should've known I couldn't tolerate finding you with someone of Nell's low caliber."

Beaver didn't say much, as influenced by Doc's

laudanum as he'd become. Ed thought he had the look of a man who was seeing an angel come visit him with the good news God wasn't ready for him yet. Beaver's eyes were rolled up in his head and he muttered mostly nonsense in reply to Mattie's pleas of love and tender mercy.

Then Ed walked her over to her room at the hotel and waited for her to throw some belongings into a kit.

"I'd do you a personal favor if you'd let me stay in town," she said rather modestly.

"You couldn't offer me nothing I couldn't buy for three dollars and not be obligated," Ed replied. "I think I'd just as soon not be beholden to you, Mattie."

"Nothing you could buy in this town would match what I could do for you, Marshal."

"I'm sure that's true. You ought to take some extra stockings, it might be cold where you're going."

"Where am I going?"

"Next stage is Denver bound, I guess that's where you'll be going."

"I never was up that way."

"Then it should be a nice experience. I reckon you can find yourself at least ten Beaver Jacks, or better'n him, up in that high-minded city."

It was maybe the wrong thing to say. Mattie cried—as Ed would later describe it to Bat—a river of tears.

## Chapter 15

———◆———

Frenchy LeBreck was toting the books when Teddy entered the Paris Club. Frenchy wore an eyeshade, garters on his sleeves. He had a stack of paper money near his right hand, a stack of silver and gold coins to his left and a tote book in the center. He was writing figures down in the book.

Teddy said, "You wanted to see me about a job."

Under the shade, Frenchy's dark gaze darted around the room. He swept the money off the table and into a cigar box, took it and the book and said, "Follow me if you please," and led Teddy to a back room where he deposited box and book in a small thick safe, then latched it shut.

"I want you to kill a man," Frenchy said, straightening from the safe.

"Who?"

"First I need some assurances you can do this thing I ask of you, that you are as you advertise yourself."

"You want me to kill someone for free to prove I can and will?"

"No, nothing so bold."

"Then what?"

"I don't know."

"A man would have to be pretty foolish to go around advertising himself as a hired gun if he wasn't one, don't you think?" Teddy said. "It's early but I could stand a drink."

Frenchy sat down behind a small desk, opened a drawer and took out a bottle half filled with amber liquid.

"Bourbon is good, yes?"

"Sure."

Frenchy held the bottle forth. Teddy took it, pulled the cork and took a decent swallow before handing it back. Frenchy's eyes never strayed from Teddy's movements.

"Where you come from, eh?"

"Does it matter?"

"I guess not. This man I want you to kill, he's very dangerous."

"They all can be, some more than others."

"How much you charge for such work?"

"Depends. If he's a high official, a lawman or politician, I charge more than if he's not. The greater the risks, the higher the fee."

"This man is no official."

"Five hundred, then."

Frenchy nodded his head approvingly.

"I guess that's okay."

"It has to be, that's what I charge."

"Okay then, when will you do it?"

"When do you want it done?"

"Soon as possible."

"Then that's when I'll do it. I still need to know who it is you want me to kill."

Frenchy took out a piece of paper and wrote a name on it and shoved it across the desk. Teddy read the name; to his surprise it wasn't either of the Mastersons. It was Bone Butcher.

"You mind my asking why you want this fellow dead?" Teddy said.

"It's personal matter. Like you say, what does it matter, eh?"

Teddy shrugged.

"Makes no difference, really."

"Good, good. I give you some of the money now and some when you finish it, eh?"

"Sure, that will be good."

Frenchy swiveled the chair about and turned the dial on the safe. It sounded like teeth clicking.

*What the hell am I going to do about this?* Teddy thought as he waited for Frenchy to retrieve half the money. Two hundred and fifty dollars in paper money is what Frenchy counted out on the desk.

"I only take gold," Teddy said.

Frenchy's brows knitted.

"I don't have that much in gold."

"When you do, let me know and I'll take care of this man."

"Okay, okay, I get it for you today. This is okay with you?"

"You know how to reach me."

Teddy turned and walked out, relieved he'd bought some time. He went to find Dog Kelly. Dog was entertaining a young robust woman at his private table in the back room of his Alhambra saloon when Teddy found him.

"We need to talk alone," Teddy stated.

Dog Kelly seemed barely to notice Teddy's presence, as fixated on the young woman as he was.

"Now," Teddy said.

Dog looked up.

"Oh, I'd like you to meet Dora Hand," Dog said. "I've just offered her work here as an entertainer."

Teddy nodded at the woman. She had violet eyes and a rosy complexion. Bunches of thick dark hair piled atop her head. Most of her stuffed into a red dress trimmed in black velvet.

"This is important, Mayor."

"Sure, sure. Dora, would you excuse us, darling?"

"Yes James," she said politely. She was sipping a liqueur.

They stepped over to a far corner out of earshot, and Teddy told Dog about the situation with Frenchy LeBreck.

"Now that's an interesting piece of news."

"Main thing is, it isn't the Mastersons he wants killed, so that leaves him out as one of your conspirators."

Dog could barely keep his attention on the problem at hand. He continued to concern himself with thoughts of Dora Hand.

"You have any ideas on what I should do about this situation?" Teddy said.

"You could always kill Bone," Dog said. "It wouldn't be any great loss to the community."

"I'll need to meet with the Mastersons," Teddy said. "As far as I'm concerned this is a situation for the law."

"Yes, you're correct, sir. I'll cogitate on it, but I got to get back to that dear sweet thing at my table lest she ply her ample services elsewhere."

Dog nodded toward Dora Hand, who offered him a little wave in return.

"Lovely . . ." Dog said and staggered off like a drunk.

Teddy went down to the city marshal's office in search of Ed and Bat, but the office was closed. He walked up the street to the Lone Star, where he found Bat sipping a cup of coffee and reading the local newspaper. Jim Masterson was at his usual station behind the bar, fresh haircut and all. Ed was playing a game of chuck-a-luck.

Teddy walked to the bar and ordered a drink, said in confidence to Jim, "I need to meet privately with Bat."

Jim nodded toward a curtain that separated the main room from a private office, said, "Go on back, I'll tell Bat."

When Bat entered a few moments later his face

showed yellowing bruises above both eyes from the fight.

Teddy told him about the situation with Frenchy LeBreck.

Bat didn't seem surprised. "Those two have been rivals since Frenchy first arrived here."

"What do you plan on doing about it?"

Bat shrugged. "I guess not much. Can't arrest a man for saying he wants somebody dead."

"He's offering five hundred dollars in gold for me to kill Bone Butcher."

"He give you any of the money yet?"

"Not yet."

"See, that's the problem in part. So far, all he's really done is talk about you killing somebody. I can't arrest somebody for mere threats. I did, half the town would be locked up."

"I suspect I'll have the money before the day's out."

"You get it, come see me or Ed. We'll go arrest Frenchy."

"He'll know I'm not who I pose myself as."

"Not my problem."

"I'm still trying to find out who wants you and your brother dead."

"Like I said before, Mr. Blue. Ed and me can handle whatever trouble comes our way. At least we know now it's not Frenchy wants us put under the sod."

"Wild Bill thought the same thing. He's buried

up in Dakota if you want to go ask him would he like a chance to reconsider his decision."

Bat's gaze narrowed.

"He was past his prime. I'm not, Ed's not either."

"I know, you're both bucking broncos that can't be broke," Teddy said and turned and walked out.

He went up to the telegraph office and sent a wire to George Bangs:

*Situation not the best. Those hired to serve uncooperative. What is latest on Horace's investigation? Wire reply soon as possible.*

*T. Blue.*

Outside the telegrapher's he rolled a shuck and smoked it and let his gaze fall upon the Bibulous Babylon. A rootin' tootin' shithole of a town cobbled out of sawn pine and windswept dreams, if ever there was one. *Its only saving grace,* he thought as he smoked down the last bit of tobacco, *is the woman who works at the Wright House.* The one he was about to go on a late autumn picnic with.

There wasn't anything to do about the Frenchy LeBreck situation but ride it out, make decisions when the time came. If he could learn who was trying to kill the Mastersons before Fenchy handed him the money, it wouldn't matter if the rest of the town learned he was a Pinkerton. If not . . . Well, he'd worry about it when that time came.

He went along the street until he came to the Wright House, found a chair out front there under the overhang, and took up residence. It was as good a place as any to watch the street, the comings and goings of the locals, and wait for Mae to get off work. He never suspected that in a matter of a few minutes he'd see a man killed over a blue shirt.

# Chapter 16

Bad Hand Frank had seen the shirt hanging in Hudson's, the haberdasher's shop window. It was the goddamnedest thing he'd ever seen. It shined.

"Sateen," Hudson said. "Just come in from San Francisco. Only one like it in all of Kansas, I suspect.

"How much?"

"Fifteen dollars."

Frank whistled.

"A man with a shirt like that would be cock of the walk. I reckon if a fancy feller like Frenchy Le-Breck or a proper man like Ted the Banker sees it, one of 'em will snap it up."

Bad Hand Frank touched it. It was soft and slick and when he touched it, light rippled through it. It had white piping across the front and pearl buttons. He could feel it begging him to buy it.

"I want me this shirt," he said impulsively.

"Fine, would you like me to wrap it, or would you just like to wear it?"

"See, that's the problem, I don't exactly have all fifteen dollars right this very second . . . on me."

"Ah well, I couldn't let it go on credit. Not this shirt. I don't suspect I'll ever get another like it. Now some of these others over here, these that are of cotton or linsey woolsey I could let go for five dollars, and maybe if you were to buy three or four, I could give you a line of credit on 'em."

This Hudson spoke with a slight lisp and wore his hair parted down the middle and slicked off to the sides and had a thin little moustache riding his upper lip. There had been rumors floated about that he had once been an actor back East and there was some question as to his manliness, or lack thereof. It irked Bad Hand Frank more than a little that Hudson wouldn't sell him that blue sateen shirt on a line of credit. He reached inside his pants pockets and dug out every last bit of money he had: seven dollars and twenty-three cents.

"That's almost half," he said.

"Not quite half exactly," Hudson said in that lisping little voice of his.

It was a most irksome situation.

"Will you hold it for me and not sell it to another if I can go and get the rest of the money?"

"I'm afraid I couldn't, with that particular shirt," Hudson said. Frank thought the way Hudson said it he was mocking him a little, letting him know that even if he had the money he might not be good enough to wear such a fancy shirt.

"You don't want me to have that shirt, isn't that it?"

Hudson shrugged. "Why should I care if you have it or not?"

"It's because of this, ain't it?" Frank held up his hand. "Because I ain't got all my parts is why you don't want me wearing it! You see this shirt on the back of a man who is whole and complete, don't you?"

"Please, Sir, you're being ridiculous."

"Well, by God I aim to go get the rest of the money and show you. I aim to own that shirt and wear it ever damn day!"

With that Frank stomped out of Hudson's and could not help, as he passed by the window, to once more glance with envy and longing at the blue sateen shirt Hudson was placing back on display, a shirt that would have Frank committing murder within the hour.

The unwitting victim of Frank's wrath happened to come along just a few minutes later. He was a pimp named Joe Hatfield who had once attended seminary school in Connecticut. This Joe Hatfield now ran a string of girls just south of the deadline, a quarter mile out of the town limits. Nobody knew why Hatfield and his girls stayed off by themselves, apart from the rest of the town. Most thought it was simply because he was unusual and did not hold truck with the more common pimps and whores of the town. He saw himself, this Joe Hatfield, as a cut above those of his ilk, and he maintained only whores of good health and nice teeth and pleasant personalities, of who now numbered five: two Dorises, a Zelda, a Juanita, and a six-foot-tall young lady named Salome.

And when Joe Hatfield came down the street that day on his mission of acquiring new dresses for said girls, he spotted that blue sateen shirt in Hudson's and promptly went in and put it on, liking instantly how it fitted him, Hudson saying, "It looks like it was made to order for you, Mr. Hatfield."

Joe Hatfield nodded with self-admiration as Hudson directed him to the full-length mirror there at the back of the shop.

"It makes you look . . ."

"Like the world's most beautiful pimp," Joe Hatfield said with mocking pride.

"Yes. I couldn't have put it better, sir. You are a lucky man to have come along when you did. Why, I almost sold it just moments ago to another."

Joe Hatfield saw the way Hudson was looking at him, with the eyes of an admiring suitor.

"Don't get any funny ideas," Joe Hatfield said. "I'm strictly a ladies' man."

Then he paid the haberdasher in hard cash and went out again, leaving his overcoat nicely unbuttoned so everyone could see the blue sateen shirt he wore.

Feeling joyful over the purchase of the shirt, Joe Hatfield made the fatal mistake of entering Bone

Butcher's drinking emporium, where stood Bad Hand Frank miserably contemplating how he was going to raise the rest of the money needed to purchase the blue shirt, the task made more difficult now that Frank had drunk up three dollars of the seven and change he'd had earlier.

It was Bone himself who made comment of Joe Hatfield's pretty shirt when Joe ordered a glass of top-shelf bourbon. It set Frank off like a rabid dog.

Teddy was sitting there in front of the Wright House when he heard gunshots, which were followed by the sight of two men running up from south of the deadline, one of them chasing the other, both men firing on the run.

Teddy instinctively stood, his hand reaching inside his coat until his fingers touched the butt of the Colt Lightning. He brought it free and held it down alongside his leg until he could discern the trouble.

From up the way he saw Bat and Ed emerge from the Lone Star, hatless, their own guns drawn.

The two men continued at a dead run down the middle of the street, folks on the sidewalks taking shelter, riders on horses spurring them out of the line of fire.

Then the lead man stumbled and fell just as he got near the front of the Wright House. His pursuer ran up to within a few feet, then stopped and aimed his piece as the other man struggled to regain his footing.

"You son of a bitch!" Frank shouted. "You went and stole my goddamn shirt!"

"It ain't your goddamn shirt, you crazy bastard, it's *my* goddamn shirt."

"Like hell. I seen it first."

"And I bought it first."

"Then buy some of this!" Frank fired off another shot, which clipped the man in the blue shirt in the knee and knocked him down again.

Bat and Ed were yelling something as they came running up from the Lone Star.

Joe Hatfield yelped in pain and snapped off a shot at Frank. The bullet took Frank's cheap hat and sent it flying off his head and Frank looked surprised. Then both men fired again simultaneously at each other.

Blue gunsmoke formed into a cloud that hung between them, waiting, it seemed, for one of those common Kansas winds to sweep it away, to lift the curtain from the drama, which oddly enough did not happen.

What were the odds that Bad Hand Frank would lose another digit to a bullet from a pimp's pistol, and that Joe Hatfield, former seminary student, would meet a quick and painless death on a frontier street so far from Connecticut?

Teddy Blue was learning fast how the frontier created its own luck for men—both good and bad.

Frank stood stung and bleeding where his forefinger had been, down as he was now to just a thumb and pinky, the blood dropping like a thick red rain, *splat, splat, spat* onto the hardpan street. He stared with disbelief at his trigger finger lying like a dead caterpillar next to his pistol.

Less fortunate lay Joe Hatfield in his blue sateen shirt now ruined by a bullet rent through its shiny front. And blossoming from the hole across the same front with its white piping was a wet red flower that spread to the neat row of pearl buttons that no longer looked so attractively fashionable. It was a shirt nobody would want to wear, not even the dead.

Frank felt much worse about the shirt than he did about the late Joe Hatfield. He reasoned hotheadedly that there was always an abundance of pimps, but like Hudson had said, that blue sateen shirt was the only one like it in all of Kansas.

Bat moved up behind Frank and touched the barrel of his Policeman's Model Colt to the back of Frank's skull.

"You're under arrest."

"I know it," Frank said sadly.

Ed said, "Why'd you shoot the pimp?"

"He stole my shirt."

"Stole his shirt," Ed repeated, looking at Bat.

Bat shook his head.

"Pimps and blue shirts," Bat said disgustedly. "This must be the week for shooting pimps."

Dog Kelly came ambling up the street, drew even with the corpse, bent to get a closer look and when satisfied, straightened and said, "It's Joe Hatfield, boys."

Bat looked around, saw Teddy still holding his pistol down along his leg.

Neither of them said anything. Bat ordered some men to take the corpse off to the undertaker's.

"I'm sure his girls will want him to have a nice funeral. I'll ride out and tell 'em."

"I'll go if you don't want to," Ed said.

"No. They're in my jurisdiction."

The brothers exchanged looks, both knowing the high quality of girls that the late pimp managed.

"We could both go," Ed suggested. "They might need more than a little comfort over such sad news."

"I guess we could both go," Bat agreed.

"Then we oughter."

There, where some of the boys had lifted away the body, was a dark stain in the dirt shaped almost like a shirt.


As Teddy and Mae sat upon the blanket, the sun low now on the horizon, its golden light spread over the land, Teddy said, "I saw a man killed over a shirt today."

Mae did not mention that she'd seen it too, from inside Wright's. She'd heard the noise and along with others had gone to look out the window just in time to see the fatal shot fired. She turned away, her own emotions at having seen yet another man murdered before her eyes too much for her.

She did not tell this lovely man whom she was

growing ever so much more fond of the dark secret she carried, and darker still was the irony of this day, this very moment, as he put his arm around her and said, "See how the sun lays upon the land. In its own way the world seems to me perfect and beautiful in spite of everything else."

And she looked and saw it too, the thing that he saw, and felt it and wanted desperately to tell him everything.

# Chapter 17

———◆———

"Elvira, honey, I'm home."

She was bathing in the sink, running a rag under her arms and around her breasts, and hadn't expected anyone to walk in on her. And when Two Bits called her name she almost screamed.

There he stood, armed to the teeth, looking haggard and hollow-eyed and smelling of whiskey and sweat and unwashed parts. She never quite figured out why she married him other than the fact he was the only man to have asked her. Her people were Pennsylvania Dutch—spare long-faced unhandsome people. Humorless and bland as porridge. She was the only girl-child, had knobby knees and offset eyes. But Two Bits had seen beauty in her other men had not, and said he'd steal the moon for her if she would marry him. She was thirty years old, no prospects looming at that age—most men considered her too old to bear children. So she married Two Bits Cline with more than a little trepidation, for he was like a wild hare. And now here he stood again, after yet another long absence from her life—coming and going like the restless Kansas wind. She never knew when he'd blow into her life, or out again.

He came all the way into the kitchen where she was washing. It wasn't a very big kitchen, although there in one corner stood a cast-iron stove that was quite luxurious by frontier standards, one he'd ordered shipped in from Kansas City for her—one of his not atypical surprises he enjoyed springing on her from time to time when he was flush. He set his rifle in one corner and took out his pistols and laid them on the table.

"You are a sight for these sore eyes of mine, Elvira."

She realized her nakedness then when his gaze fell on her, and took a towel and covered herself, but it didn't stop him from staring at that portion of her.

"I've had a lust in my heart for you ever since I left Montana," he said. There was just something about killing that made him feel carnal. In fact, he had stopped at a whorehouse in Billings and spent nearly a hundred dollars of the money he'd gotten to shoot the Pepper twins. The money paid to him by the boys' own step-mamma.

It surprised Two Bits how such a pretty woman could have a heart cold enough to pay to have her stepsons shot dead, how coolly she had negotiated the entire transaction, as though bartering with him to shingle a roof or dig a well.

"You're awfully pretty to be dallying in such ugly business," Two Bits had said to her.

"What has my beauty got to do with anything?" she said. Her name, he thought she said, was Lucille.

"I guess nothing," Two Bits said.

She'd talked him down from his usual thousand dollars to just six hundred, using a good bit of expensive whiskey and more than a few of her charming smiles, which hinted at greater rewards to come if he did the job "right and fast."

"Oh, it'll be done proper," he assured her. "I'm very good at what I do."

"So am I," she said, this Lucille.

And so off he'd gone and found the Pepper twins and shot them. And he met Mosely and his whorish wife and watched her rob the dead boys and felt sorry for Mosely and would have killed the whorish wife for free if Mosely would have asked him to, so sorry for the man did Two Bits feel. Two Bits was glad he had a wife who wasn't whorish in nature, but as he looked at Elvira standing there with just a towel to cover her breasts that reminded him of white pears, she seemed to him a seductress. He craved her bad. But even in his craving he thought about the one woman he didn't get: Lucille.

After he shot the boys and he was about to ride back to the big house where this Lucille—current second wife of the elder Pepper—resided, Two Bits got word the law was looking for him, that they knew his exact name and description and everything about him. Two Bits realized then how the law learned such intimate details. He recalled this Lucille saying how good she was at what she did, which was obviously betrayal.

So instead he rode all the way to Billings with this cruel lust eating at him, swearing as he went that he ought to save such lust for his dear wife, Elvira. But lust is a powerful thing, and Billings was as far as Two Bits could go before giving in to it.

The girls he had in Billings were fat and wore bored expressions while he took his pleasure with them. But still the respite made it some easier riding on back down to Kansas, and now next to the pistols on the table he placed what remained of his shooting money—some four hundred dollars and change.

"I had me a good month," Two Bits said. "Why don't you drop that towel and come over and say hidy."

As a Christian woman, Elvira felt the slightest sting of insult by such crude suggestions. However, she'd come to prize Two Bits for what he was by nature and was slightly titillated by his ways, especially after such long absences. It amazed her how much he lusted after her. He looked overall like something horses had dragged over the prairies. He had not one handsome trait about him. She did not know why she loved him, she only knew that she did.

And later as they lay on the sunlit floor of the

not-very-large kitchen, the soles of Two Bits' feet touching the cold iron legs of the stove, Two Bits felt whole and human again and so did Elvira. They both knew there was a long winter ahead of them.

"I've got to ride over to Dodge and shoot some more folks," he said.

"See, that's the part about you I care least about," she said. "The fact you shoot people for a living. I wish you'd give up that sort of work and find something regular and less dangerous."

"It's all I know to do," he said. "It's all I've ever known how to do."

"But someday something will go wrong and it will be you who gets shot or captured and hanged by the law. And I'll be a widow and no better off than I was before you married me."

"Well, when that day comes, I'll worry about it and you should too, but not until that day comes."

"It will be too late."

"Oh, it ain't ever too late to worry," Two Bits said.

He looked at the sunlight streaming through the windows and it caused him to squint at how bright it was. "I bet that is what heaven looks like," he said. "Just like that old sun, bright and shiny like a new dollar. I bet it never rains in heaven and it never gets cold and the wind don't ever blow like it does here in Kansas."

She looked at the light too. Beyond the panes of glass, she could see the clouds had parted, the rays of sun beaming through to come all the way down into the small kitchen. If she stretched out her hand far enough, she could touch the sun there on the floor, feel its warmth.

She didn't want to say to him what she was thinking: that assassins most likely would never get to know what it was like in heaven or anything close to it. Heaven was no place for assassins or men who lusted after women, and it made her sad to think that when she died and when Two Bits died they'd never meet again in heaven.

"When will you be going to Dodge?" she said.

Without his clothes, and with the exceptions of his hands and face and part of his neck, Two Bits was as white all over as a fish's belly, whereas Elvira was more evenly colored.

"Soon as my needs is slaked," he said.

"You hungry?"

"For everything you got, Elvira darling."

"You talk so wicked," she said.

"I know it."

"You could have been anything in life you'd wanted to be, I imagine," she said.

"I know it."

"It's a shame you took the wrong path."

"They's four hundred dollars on that table for a few minutes' work," Two Bits said. "I don't know what other path I could have taken that would have paid me so well."

"Money isn't everything."

"You tell me what is, I'll go do it."

"I wish we'd met when we were both young so we could have had babies," she said.

"Babies," Two Bits said, the thought of having little ones forming in his mind. He wondered exactly who the babies would look like: him or Elvira. Them poor kids would have been ugly, he reasoned.

"We may have to move down to Mexico for a while," he said, wanting to change the subject of babies.

"I like it just fine right here."

"These men I've got to go shoot," he said. "It might make it tough to stay in Kansas or anyplace close after I shoot 'em."

She thought about the chore of packing their belongings, about the heartbreak of leaving yet another place she'd settled into. She thought about long days of journeying to new places she knew nothing about, about trying to ingratiate herself into such places. She thought about seeing Two Bits hanging from a tree, a rope around his scrawny unwashed neck, his hands hanging limp at his sides, the Kansas wind twisting him around and around. She thought about crows eating his eyes and shuddered.

There could be no good coming from such an outlaw life. But the prairies were a lonely far-flung place, and a body had to do whatever a body could to survive for however long God appointed to each poor soul, hers included.

"Let's go it again," Two Bits said. "Then after, you can fix me a nice plate of grub whilst I clean my guns."

She closed her eyes and felt his weight lower onto her, knowing that it would not be too many more times that she would feel such a thing—that their appointed time was growing short and soon there would be no weight at all, no white flesh, no startling eyes searching for her hidden beauty . . .

. . . and heard the windsong along the eaves like a whisper, mournful, like a sad old choir of the long lost voices of all those who had passed before and were now crying out their warning. And when the wind rattled the bare branches of a lone cottonwood that scraped and clicked against the window glass, it sounded like bones rattling.

Two Bits stuck the whole ride.

# Chapter 18

————•••————

Mae and Teddy made their way back to Dodge just after sunset, a silver light still playing in the westerly sky but the land growing full of dark now.

"You feeling like me?" he said.

"In what way?"

"That I hate to see this evening come to an end."

"Yes," she said.

"There's an opera house," he suggested.

"I'd love to go."

"Eddie Foy is playing there. I saw it on the playbill earlier."

"It would be such a nice way to spend the evening."

"Afterward we could . . ."

"Yes, I was thinking the same thing."

He liked very much how her thoughts seemed to coincide with his own. It was a little spooky.

"Drop me off so I can freshen and change clothes," she said.

They agreed on a time that he would come

around and pick her up and sealed it with a light kiss. He waited until she went into the boarding house before he returned the cab and horse to the stables.

He was walking back up from the stables toward his hotel when he encountered Frenchy LeBreck.

"I've been looking for you," Frenchy said.

"You found me."

"I have the money."

"Let's go in and have a drink."

"It is not necessary. Here." Frenchy took a small leather purse from his coat and handed it to Teddy.

"Two hundred dollars in gold double eagles. I'll get you the rest when it is finished, eh?"

Teddy hefted the purse.

"Let's get a drink, I feel like having a drink."

Frenchy seemed reluctant. "I have to go meet someone," he said. "When will you do it?"

"A time and place of my choosing."

"It must be done soon."

"Okay, I'll do it soon."

"Good, good. I go now. You come see me when you've done it."

Teddy watched him stalk off toward the dead-line, saw the shadows swallow him like the black maw of a monster that ate men with dark hearts.

He went to find one of the Mastersons to give him the money and wash his own hands of the affair.

He checked first at the city marshal's office. It

was closed. He went down to the Lone Star. Jim was the only Masterson in attendance.

"I'm trying to locate Bat and Ed," Teddy said.

Jim was like the rest of them—dark eyes that held a combination of wariness and amusement.

"I ain't seen either of 'em in the last couple of hours."

"You expect them in? It's important."

"I think they went off looking for some stole horses."

"Let me have a whiskey."

Jim poured it with hands as smooth as porcelain and set it there on the oak.

"Ed and Bat told me the story on you," Jim said. "I just want you to know, I think Dog did the right thing sending for you."

Teddy nodded, sipped his drink. "They probably told you too then, word can't get out about who I am."

Jim nodded. "Mastersons never look for trouble," he said. "But we don't ever run from it either. They've got nothing against you personally, it's just that they like to fight their own fights."

"What about you?"

"Oh hell, I like to fight my own fights too, I'm just not a fighter like them. I prefer the pursuit of business—you know, make everyone happy, give 'em what they want if they're willing to pay for it."

"Well, nobody's asking anybody to run."

"I just wanted you to know I'm not against the

idea of your being here to help us out. You need anything from me, just ask."

"I'll remember that."

Jim nodded, said, "Here comes Dog sporting a new gal."

Teddy turned, saw Dog Kelly and his new employee, Dora Hand. Dog had dusted off his beaver hat and slapped a shine on his coat and shoes and looked like a grandee. Dora looked elegant as only a slightly aging chanteuse could. Her face was powdered to a rare whiteness and she had a dark little mole the size of a raisin there at the corner of her mouth alongside the very red painted lips.

Dog looked like he was about to burst out of his waistcoat with pride.

"Boys!" he announced loudly enough for everyone in the place to hear. "Like you all to meet the new singer here in town, Miss Dora Hand."

Dora smiled in a queenly way.

Jim licked his lips.

Dog ordered Dora a liqueur and himself a cocktail.

"Could I have a word with you in private?" Teddy said while they waited for Jim to mix their drinks.

Dog looked disappointed to have his lovely time interrupted with business. He led Dora to a table and pulled the chair out for her, then scooted it back in again as Jim brought over their drinks.

"Well, we just stopped in before going to the opera," Dog said.

"It's about that situation with Frenchy."

"Excuse me for one moment, my dear."

Teddy and Dog walked off a few steps.

"What's new on that situation?" Dog liked talking in terms that spoke of situations.

"Frenchy gave me a down payment to kill Bone," Teddy said, tapping the purse of gold in his coat pocket."

"You talked to Bat and Ed about it?"

"Bat wanted me to get the money so he could arrest Frenchy. I got half the money but Bat's off chasing after stolen nags somewhere."

Dog squinted in his deliberation.

"I could deputize you and—"

"No good if you still want me to maintain my secrecy and find out who's out to assassinate the Mastersons."

"Well, just stall for time, wait until Bat and Ed get back."

"Frenchy wants it done soon."

"He say why he's in an all-hell-fire hurry to get Bone dead and in the ground?"

"Who knows?"

Dog saw Jim lingering around Dora's table, chatting amiably with her and she with him and it made him feel itchy because Jim was a nice-looking man with the charm of a faro dealer.

"I got to get back over there or old Jim will be

bedding her before I ever get to hear her sing a single note."

"You learn anything more on your end about who it is wants Ed and Bat dead?"

"I got it narrowed down to either Angus Bush or Bone Butcher. Course you was to kill Bone for Frenchy, that would take care of some of it." Dog smiled at the half joke, said, "I trust you'll know what to do, Mr. Blue, gotta go."

Teddy left the Lone Star and walked down to Bone Butcher's.

The night, as nights went in a rip-roaring town like Dodge, was young yet, but already the Silk Garter seemed in full swing. The Garter was a place where a man could buy just about anything he could at any of the other saloons and dance halls south of the Deadline, it was just that a man could buy things cheaper at Bone's place. You could taste it in the watered-down liquor that sold for a nickel a glass less than the other places. You could hear it in the clack of the roulette wheel that wouldn't take a genius to figure out it was probably rigged so a gambler would win one out of every thirty times instead of one out of every twenty. You could tell it in the weary expressions of the aging dance-hall queens who were only one cut above the crib girls.

Bone was there at a table gambling with four other men. Beneath his derby resided a broad flat face that had a fighter's nose. He laughed louder than everyone else, and talked louder. He had a presence about him that dominated and cowed the others around him. He was a man of force, somebody that would go the whole line with you if you got him riled. He was the type of man that you'd better be prepared to kill if you got into a fight with him. He had priggish eyes bereft of any human kindness.

Teddy studied the man long enough to understand what he thought he needed to know about him. Then just as he was about to walk out of the place, he saw Bone rise suddenly from the table and go quickly to a woman standing at the bar and take hold of her roughly.

There were words exchanged between them, words that were lost in the din and cacophony of the crowd. He saw Bone slap the woman hard enough to snap her head to the side. Nobody tried to intervene. He saw the woman run out the back door holding the side of her face. Bone walked back to his table and joined his game, laughing, as though he'd just gone over to squash a cockroach he'd seen crawling along the bar. As though it meant no more to him than that—to slap a woman.

Teddy left the place. He'd seen all of Bone Butcher he wanted to see. Such a man probably deserved killing by someone at some time or place, but Teddy told himself he wasn't going to be the one to do it, in spite of what he'd just seen.

He crossed the street and was walking toward the Paris Club when he saw the woman that Bone Butcher had violated enter a side door. Then it dawned on him why Frenchy wanted Bone dead.

Love was as good a reason as any to kill for—perhaps better than most. At least killing for love seemed somehow noble.

He figured it was time to go clean up and pick up Mae for the opera house. Let the night have its sinners and injustices. There was always tomorrow to confess and seek forgiveness and right the wrongs.

There would still be heaven and there'd still be Dodge City.

# Chapter 19

Charlotte's daddy was beat black and blue still, but the old man had forgiven the boys for their ill behavior, so glad was he to have his eldest daughter married off—even to a man of Buck Pierce's caliber. Charlotte's daddy figured that, when Buck wasn't drinking or stealing or doing some of the other illegal activity he and Hannibal often got involved in, he wasn't that bad a feller. He treated Charlotte right, never abused her, and once she was married, the old man figured Charlotte would give up the whoring profession and restore what little honor there had been to the Myers family name.

They all stood around the yard waiting for the circuit preacher to arrive, Dirty Dave Rudabaugh among them. Charlotte's women kin had decorated tables and laden them with all manner of food. Some of the men had brought homemade whiskey in crocks and a barrel of ice beer. Kids ran around the yard like wild Indians. The ground where there was still shade from the outbuildings held frost from the night before.

Hannibal and Buck and Dirty Dave stood together, the wind tugging at their coats.

"This is a funny time of year to get married," Dirty Dave said, looking up at the smoky sky. It was a chill wind that tugged at their coats and at Dirty Dave's long brutish moustaches: icy, with the breath of winter in it.

Hannibal and Buck looked at Dave when he said that it was a funny time of year to get married.

"Why's it funny?" Hannibal said.

"Just seems most folks get married in the spring or summer is all. Hardly nobody gets married this late in the year. It's dang near winter. Why I wouldn't be surprised if it don't snow before the day is out."

Buck and Hannibal looked up at the sky. They didn't see any snow.

The elder Myers came over, his face blotchy with bruises. He wore his hat gentle on his head because of the sore knots the boys had raised on it beating him. He walked with a slight limp too, from where they kicked him some.

"I'm sure sorry about the other night," Buck said. "I don't know what got into us."

"Bad liquor is what got into you boys," Myers said, but then quickly added: "Course, you boys is yet young and wild and I know what that's like. I was that-a-way myself once. I'm pure ashamed at some of the things I did in my youth. Weddings is a time to bury hatchets and forget the past and that's what I aim to do. All is forgiven."

"Have a drink, sir," Hannibal said, offering a jug of homebrew that one of the guests had brought.

Myers looked at him.

"I don't think we should start to drinking until after the ceremony. You know how you boys get when you drink."

Hannibal and Buck nodded their heads.

"Not me," Dirty Dave said. "I don't get no way when I drink except happy." He took hold of the jug and took a long pull from it. "Tastes like glory," he said.

Hannibal and Buck were about to break down and taste some of the glory too when somebody shouted the preacher was coming. They could see him there across the broad lifeless prairies. Riding a switch-tail mule looking like Moses crossing the wilderness.

Buck could feel his heart quicken a little. He looked over at Charlotte, who was wearing a wedding dress her mama had given her from her own trousseau; the dress was a bit snug in some places that Hannibal and Dave took secret pleasure in admiring.

Buck said, "I best go out and meet that preacher."

"I'll go with you," Charlotte's daddy said.

And when they'd walked out to meet the preacher Hannibal said, "I'm sure enough sorry to see 'em get married."

"Why's that?" Dirty Dave asked.

"Charlotte was the best whore in Mister. I'm sure going to miss buying her."

"After we rob that fat bank in Dodge you can buy any whore you want."

Hannibal looked a bit forlorn.

"Hand me that jug, would you?"

Dave handed it to him and Hannibal took a nice swallow. "I know it," he said, wiping his mouth with the cuff of his coat. "But they ain't a one I could buy would be good as her in some ways."

"What sort of ways?" Dave asked curiously.

Hannibal looked at him hard. "I reckon we ought to respect the fact it's her wedding day. Maybe someday I'll tell you, but that there's my friend she's marrying and it would be wrong to get into it, I reckon."

Dave took another swallow of the liquor and then Hannibal took another and said, "Listen, I start any fighting, bash me over the head with your pistol barrel will you?"

The preacher rode in and dismounted and took his bible from his saddle pockets. He wore no hat, so his hair blew long and wild from his head like gray streamers. He was tall and gangly and when he wasn't preaching he was the undertaker there in Mister and took in the dead and got them ready for their last long journey. His name was Haggard.

"Boys, I just rode from Dreary, where I buried two little infant children dead of the influenza. And it's been a long hard day for me already, so if you all don't mind, let's get this wedding under way, because I am about starved to the bone and dry as a nail for a taste of something wet."

Charlotte wept throughout the ceremony and Buck looked dazed. Some of the women wept too, and the men who weren't related and one or two who were—somewhat distantly so—felt more than a few pangs of regret that the best whore in Mister was now getting married off. There were only two whores left in that little burg, and one had the consumption and the other was cross-eyed and hard to look at.

It was a quick wedding and soon enough folks were seated around the tables grabbing fried chicken and cooked okra and boiled turnips and the like. Then it began to snow and there they all sat eating like there was no tomorrow and that Jesus might come anytime and call their number with the snow falling in their hair, and Dirty Dave thought, *Goddamn, maybe it was a mistake or a bad sign or something, that snow*, but nonetheless, the liquor was good and hard and by the time the snow had grown three, four inches deep, he didn't notice it anymore.

The preacher got drunk and they put him in the cellar with a few warm blankets and fed and watered his old mule. Buck of course went off with his bride to Mister to the one hotel, since there was little room in the house. Hannibal and Dirty Dave slept on the kitchen floor.

They were lying there near the stove, the cherry glow of its fire upon their drunken faces.

"What's that?" Hannibal said, listening.

"Sounds like a cat mewing off somewheres," Dave said.

"Like it's got its paw caught in a trap or something."

"Yeah, sounds just like a hurt cat, don't it?"

They listened to the sounds and it spooked them some.

Then Dirty Dave caught on to what it was making those sounds and began giggling like a schoolgirl and Hannibal said, "What the shit you giggling at?" and Dirty Dave said, "Don't you get it, what's making them sounds?"

"No, but I'm by God about ready to get my boots on and ride to Mister just to get away from 'em."

"It's . . . it's . . ." Dirty Dave couldn't hardly get the words out.

"It's what?"

"It's the old man in there with the mama," Dirty Dave said.

"Oh . . ." Then Hannibal started giggling too.

"Goddamn, you believe old folks like that doing it?"

"No . . ."

*Giggle, giggle.*

"Listen at 'em."

"I'm listening."

*Giggle, giggle.*

"Shsssh . . . they'll hear and the old man will come and pitch us out in the snow."

And the snow fell silent and for a long time, and Buck Pierce and Charlotte did not arrive back at the house for two days. And when they did arrive, some of the glow had worn off Buck's face from the last time the boys got a look at him helping his new bride into the wagon to take her off for a honeymoon at the Mister hotel.

Dirty Dave and Hannibal were feeding the horses and breaking ice plates out of the water buckets when Buck wandered over and said, "Boys, I'm about ready to get into the wind, how about you-all?"

"We been ready," Dirty Dave said.

"How was it, the honeymooning part?" Hannibal said.

Buck just looked at him and said, "It was about like before."

Dave said, "You all ready to go kill them Mastersons and get to that fat bank?"

Buck looked off toward the house where Charlotte had gone inside.

"Boys, I ain't so sure I'm husband material," he said.

"Fellers like us never was meant to be the marrying kind," Dirty Dave said. "I could have told you that much. Why, we got feet made of feathers."

"You done gone and got poetical ways," Hannibal said.

"You boys been in the whiskey again, ain't you?" Buck said.

They giggled, still thinking about the sounds

they had heard last night, the mewing sounds
Buck's daddy had made with his mama, then sad-
dled their horses and mounted them and Dave
said, "You want to go kiss your bride good-bye
before we leave on out of here? It might be a long
time before we come back this way."

Buck said, "No, I guess I kissed her enough these
last couple of days to last me a month or two."

"Well, let's burn daylight."

So that's what they did, they burned daylight.
And when Charlotte came out to see where her
new husband was, all she saw were horse tracks in
the snow heading off toward the east, and those
tracks looked like they were only headed one way
and weren't ever going to be heading any other.

Her mama came out and stood next to her and
they both stared off at the pewter sky and empty
landscape that went all the way to the sky.

"Men . . ." Charlotte said forlornly.

But Charlotte's mama only smiled a knowing
smile. Men were the biggest mystery God had ever
made. A mystery she'd stopped trying to figure
out forty years ago. "They are what they are," she
said.

A whistling wind chased them both back inside.

# *Chapter 20*

————◆————

After that night's performance at the opera house, Dog invited everyone to his Alhambra for cocktails and a feast. Dog had it in mind to ask Dora's hand in marriage. Among the honored guests were Eddie Foy, the famous comedian who had been the main entertainment that evening; Bat and Ed Masterson, who'd arrived back early enough for the last half of the show; Teddy and Mae; and Dora Hand, of course.

Dog was magnanimous in his hosting, having had his barkeep set out a spread of food fit for a king, including fresh oysters, mussels, catfish, steaks big as dinner plates, hams, cakes and pies, his best bonded whiskey, and cocktails.

"You certainly know how to put on the dog, Mayor," the comic said. Dog thought it funny, that expression, added it to his personal collection of sayings and witticisms.

Teddy waited until the right moment, then got Bat's attention when they went to the bar to get cocktails for some of the others.

"Frenchy paid me half the money," Teddy said.

"Then that's good enough for me to arrest him."

"Maybe you could just talk to him, let him know that you know what he's planning. I don't think he's dangerous."

"Never knew a Pinkerton to have sympathy for criminals."

"He's no criminal. He's doing it over a woman being abused by Bone. I saw Bone work her over tonight, saw her go straight to Frenchy's."

"The Rose," Bat said. "Should have known it was something along those lines. The only thing that surprises me is that Bone didn't hire you to kill Frenchy instead of the other way around. Or, that Bone didn't kill Frenchy himself."

"I doubt he knows."

"I do too. Bone's one jealous sucker."

"What do you want to do?"

Bat looked at the drinks mixed by the barkeep.

"Tonight, nothing. I'm tired from running down horse thieves and train robbers and seeing dead bodies and all the rest. I'd like to enjoy myself for one solitary evening. I'll go see Frenchy in the morning. You got the money with you?"

Teddy reached in his pocket, took out the purse and handed it to Bat.

Bat hefted its weight.

"Money and women and jealousy," he said. "Bad concoction." Then he took up the cocktails and walked them over to the table and set them down.

Mae came to the bar just as Bat walked away

and said, "Maybe we should leave, go someplace a little less crowded."

She had a smile that brought him comfort.

"Yeah, maybe we should."

"Your place?"

"That's what I was thinking."

"Me too."

It was sometime during the night, maybe early morning before daylight when someone pounded on the door. Teddy tumbled from the bed, leaving the warmth of Mae, reaching for his pistol as he did.

She started to ask what was happening but he touched her lips with his finger.

"Who is it?" he said through the closed door.

"It's me, Dog Kelly . . ."

He opened the door. Dog was standing there looking glum, red-eyed.

"What's going on?"

"Somebody shot and killed my sweet Dora . . ."

Dog nearly collapsed into the room. Teddy took hold of him and sat him in a chair. Dog was in tears as he told the story of how a rider came past his place twenty minutes earlier and fired into the little line shack he kept out back of the Alhambra.

"She was in my bed sleeping. I guess whoever shot her thought it was me in there asleep. Poor, poor child . . ."

Dog blubbered his heartache, finally got the words out that Bat and Ed were after the shooter.

"They know who it was?"

"It's that Kennedy kid," Dog said. "He's been wanting me dead since I whipped him like a pup for rowdyism in my place last summer. His daddy owns the biggest ranch in Texas. Oh, gawd!"

Mae discreetly dressed and poured Dog a drink and he looked at her and bawled all the more, remembering what beauty was and how fatal it could be, and his tears fell onto her hands as she held his to help steady the glass.

"She's gone!" Dog wailed. "My sweet Dora's gone!"

It was a full day before the Mastersons returned to Dodge with the boy in tow, his right arm shattered by one of Bat's bullets.

"Lock that peckerwood up," Bat told Ed. "And if he tries anything, shoot him in the goddamn face like he shot Dora."

Teddy had seen them ride in, and walked over to the office.

The kid, Kennedy, was just that, a petulant-looking boy who probably never knew what a lick of work felt like. He had wild black curls that sprawled from under his broad hat and chaps that had silver conchos stitched down the seams. He had dull unhappy eyes. Ed shoved him in a cell and slapped the door shut and locked it. The boy sat on the cot and knuckled his hat back from his forehead with his good arm, said, "I need a doctor, you busted my arm."

"Ought to let you bleed out," Bat said. "You churlish little bastard."

Dog got word and came running over to the jail, his face red with anger and weeping half the night.

"Let me at him!"

Ed held him off. "He'll get a trial."

"Forget the trial, let me at him."

"Can't do it, you know that, Dog."

"Then you're fired."

"You can't fire me."

Dog made a feeble attempt to grab Bat's pistol but Bat slapped his hand away, said, "Go on home, Dog. Go get a drink or something. He'll get his comeuppance. Let the law handle it."

Teddy noticed the boy's expression never changed so much as a tick. He sat there as though waiting for a train to come, his hand-tooled boots crossed at the ankles.

"Why'd you do it?" Dog shouted. "Why'd you shoot poor Dora?"

This was when the boy looked up.

"Meant to shoot you, old man. Never meant to shoot no woman."

Of course none of them could have known then that the boy's justification would be good enough for a jury to acquit him several months later and let him ride back down to the biggest ranch in Texas with nothing more than a bunged-up arm that had one of Bat Masterson's bullets in it.

"He'll hang for sure, Dog," Ed said.

Bat nodded his agreement.

"Ain't a jury in the state won't find him guilty."

They just didn't know that twelve men would see a different logic: that the kid wasn't aiming to kill Dora but Dog, and if it wasn't his intent to kill her, it was an accident. Dog would say after the acquittal that justice hadn't been blind that day, that "she had her dang eyes poked out with a rich man's stick!"

But at the time there was only the sorrowful news to deal with, the business of burial at hand.

Wind swept hard out of the north as the funeral cortege wound its way toward the cemetery outside of Dodge. Dog had ordered a fine headstone of marble from a Kansas City stonemason, but it would not arrive for three weeks. A couple of the boys dug a grave with picks and shovels. The ground was already growing hard from the cold nights. Dog paid for a new dress for Dora to be buried in: a black gown of mourning to match his black mourning suit. He paid for the finest casket the town had: a polished rosewood coffin with silver handles. The undertaker Haggard did prepare the lovely corpse, placing a think lace veil of black over Dora's beautiful features. *She's a beauty,* the mortician thought, almost desirous.

Dora rode stately as a queen in the big glass-sided Sayers and Scovill hearse pulled by a matched pair of Morgans. Dog rode his bay alongside, weeping every step of the way, big cold tears rolling down his cheeks.

Teddy and Mae rode in their rented cab behind

the brass band Dog had hired to play the dirge. Half the townspeople turned out for the affair, the other half did not. The more respectable citizens, those who resided north of the deadline, saw little reason to attend the funeral of another dead prostitute. Dead prostitutes were a common event in Dodge and some of those self-respecting types saw no cause to give either credence or respect to a fallen cyprian.

Small flakes of snow fell from the sky in a lazy manner, like it wasn't in any more of a hurry to touch the ground and become lost than were the newly dead.

"It's so sad," Mae said.

And it was sad, the way she said it, and made the whole situation feel even sadder.

"You ever lose anyone you loved?" Teddy asked.

"Yes," she said.

"Me too."

She touched his arm. The wind blew. The procession came to the cemetery. Dora was buried. The day was half over.

Trouble was on its way.

# Chapter 21

———⊙———

Frenchy was waiting outside Teddy's hotel. "We need to talk," he said.

"I'll come around to your place in a bit. I've got to see my company home."

Frenchy looked at Mae. "He's found out, Bone has gotten word somehow."

"Go and wait for me at your place."

"You come soon, eh?"

"Yes."

Frenchy stalked off.

"What was that about?" Mae said as Teddy helped her from the cab.

"Some odd business. Can I walk you back to the Wright House?"

"No, you go ahead, take care of your odd business. Come around later when you're finished."

He kissed her lightly on the mouth feeling the need to do just that in light of the events of the day. "I'm glad we met each other," he said.

"I am too."

They stood for a moment, each searching for that indescribable something in the other's eyes.

"There are things I want to ask you about yourself," he said.

"I know," she said. "And things I need to tell you about."

He saw something pass through her, something that turned her eyes sad.

"Go on, we'll talk later," she said.

He walked down to the Paris Club and was directed to the back room, where he found Frenchy pacing nervously.

"He will kill me if you don't kill him first," Frenchy uttered.

"I can't kill him."

"*Mon dieu!* Why not?"

"Tell me why you want him dead."

"What does it matter?"

"Is it because of the woman?"

Frenchy stopped pacing.

"How you know about her?"

"I saw her come here the other night after Bone slapped her around."

Frenchy stopped pacing.

"Yes it is because of her, how he treats her. If someone doesn't stop him, then he will kill her someday and she will be buried like that other one and she will be just one more that nobody cares about. But I care! I care enough to kill him myself if you won't do it."

"I can't kill him, because I'm not who I represented myself as. I'm no assassin."

"Then why you—"

"I can't explain it right now, but I've got a job I need to do and it was one way of doing it, passing myself off as a gun for hire."

"Then I will kill him . . ."

"And if he kills you, how will that protect the woman?"

Frenchy sagged into the chair behind his desk.

"You don't understand, how it is I feel about her."

"Take her and leave Dodge if you love her that much."

"I can't, everything I own is here in this place. Besides, why should I run?"

"Your choice, my friend, but there's nothing I can do for you. I've told the sheriff about the situation. He has the money you gave me. He'll be around later to talk to you."

"You have betrayed me."

"Yeah, I guess maybe I have, but that wasn't my intent." Teddy felt sorry as hell for the little man, but he'd done all that he could for him. The rest would have to be left to someone else.

He met Bat Masterson on the way out.

"I've already told him what the situation is," Teddy said.

"I should arrest him but I'm running out of cells, what with the horse thieves me and Ed arrested, that kid who shot Dora, and Bad Hand Frank."

"Wait until Frenchy does something worth ar-resting him for."

"Like killing Bone?"

"He's no match for Bone Butcher."

"I should run 'em both out of town."

"Others like 'em will take their place."

"Hell. Least I ought to fine him some of this money," Bat said, taking the purse from his pocket.

"Dog thinks it's narrowed down to Bone Butcher or Angus Bush who wants you and your brother dead."

"He's probably about right on that score."

"Give me another day or two to see what I can find out, okay?"

Bat looked at him. "I guess it doesn't matter one way or the other. If it's not one of them, it'll be somebody else sooner or later. The law is like rain, it falls on those who want it and those who don't. South of that deadline nobody wants it. We'll see who wins out."

Teddy walked away. The snow was falling nicely now, steady and covering the fresh grave of Dora Hand in a lovely mantle of white just as it was covering the town of Dodge. Teddy longed for the warmth of the Mexican sun, a cool place in the shade of some adobe, sitting down there with John, drinking tequila and listening to the music in the plaza. It would be nice to be back down there with a woman like Mae—a place where the living was easy and practically nobody wanted to kill anybody.

He walked up the street and into the Silk Garter.

"Bone Butcher around?"

The barkeep was wiping out glasses with a stained rag.

"Back in his room," the barkeep said, pointing with his chin.

Teddy started back.

"I wouldn't I was you."

"Why not?"

"He's got company. He don't like being disturbed when he's got company."

"Too bad."

The barkeep started to come around the end of the bar. He was a good-size, solid-built Dutchman. Teddy hit him with a solid right cross that exploded against the side of his head. The Dutchman went down, started to rise, sank back again and rolled over. It was a blow, if delivered right, that struck the temple and knocked a man cold.

Teddy continued down the hall until he heard Bone's voice coming from behind one of the doors. He kicked it open and walked in, pistol aimed.

The Rose was tied facedown to the bed, naked from the waist up. Red lash marks striped her back and Bone was holding a buggy whip, ready to put a few more stripes on her.

"What the hell—"

"Put it down and untie her."

"Get the hell out of here!"

Teddy thumbed back the hammer, saw Bone's piggish eyes settle on the black maw aimed at his middle.

"From what I hear, the funeral party would be small," Teddy said.

"What funeral party?"

"Yours."

Bone's whip hand lowered.

"You the son of a bitch Frenchy hired to kill me."

"That's about right."

"Go ahead if you're up to it."

Teddy stepped in quick, brought the steel barrel of the Colt down hard across Bone's forehead, splitting it open nearly as clean as if he had slashed him with a straight razor. Bone fell away from the blow grabbing handfuls of blood.

Teddy stood over him, the barrel just inches from his face.

"Get a real close look, it might just be the last thing you see."

Bone made a movement and Teddy hit him again, this time across the collarbone, then pressed the barrel of the revolver to the bloody wound.

"Just so you know," he said. "I gave Frenchy his money back, but I still got six lead pills for that headache you're developing if you want them. Now untie the woman."

Teddy stepped aside while Bone struggled to untie the Rose, drops of his blood falling on her bare back and mixing with the bloody stripes. Once untied, she grabbed a robe and shucked it on and looked at Teddy as she huddled against the door.

"Go on," he said, and she went.

"Now what?" Bone said.

"You let her go and you leave Frenchy alone."

Bone shook his head defiantly.

"I don't let no woman go once she belongs to me."

Teddy shot him in the foot, watched him hop and fall.

"Just so you understand my position on this," he said to Bone.

Bone cringed in his newly found pain.

"You shot my toes off!"

"There are worse things than toes you could get shot off. And I'm sure there are other women you can find to abuse. Just not that one, understood?"

Bone lay there like a wounded dog, defeated by a bigger meaner dog. It was enough. Teddy lowered the pistol.

"Remember," he said. "Frenchy and the woman are off-limits."

Ed was coming through the doors of the Silk Garter just as Teddy was going out.

"I heard a gunshot."

"Bone had an accident."

"He dead?"

"No."

"Bat told me the situation about the deal Frenchy had with you . . ."

"I didn't come here because of that."

"He need a doctor?" Ed said, glancing toward the long hallway at the back of the bar.

"I reckon he will."

"Self defense, you say?"

"Accident."

Ed nodded. The two parted company, went their separate ways, Teddy not sure exactly how he was feeling about what happened, but not feeling overly bad about it either. He stopped down at the telegraph office to check for messages. There wasn't any. He stopped at the post office and a letter from John marked GENERAL DELIVERY was waiting for him.

*Old pard. Life down here isn't as good as when you were still hanging around. Hell, I'm about ready to die of boredom. When you finishing up and heading back? I was thinking maybe we could go into the cow business. It's something we both know and these Mexican beeves run wild out in the chaparral—it wouldn't take much to get us a small herd started and it'd beat robbing banks. I'm about ready to settle down to a steady life. Besides that, I got a situation brewing with you know who. She's been coming around and I been doing my best to ignore her. I think she knows the padre is*

*growing restless too since he seen you leave.*
*Think she's afraid he'll leave her behind. I*
*tried to tell her different, but she's taken to*
*me like a pup. It'd be nice to have an amigo*
*to talk to and get some good advice. Don't*
*know how much longer I can stay here if you*
*ain't intending to return. Are you? Let me*
*know.*

*John S.*

Teddy couldn't help but smile. John, he had a
way of drawing trouble to him like flies to a dung
heap.

# Chapter 22

———◆———

Wolves howled when they caught wind of him. Two Bits looked off into the moon-struck night made brighter still by the freshly fallen snow. Ahead a mile he could see the lights of Dodge twinkling like stars that had frozen and fallen to earth. It felt brutal cold, but work lay just ahead. A thousand dollars' worth of work if Bone Butcher hadn't gone and hired someone else, or if someone hadn't already killed the Masterson Brothers.

Someday, he told himself, he'd like to visit the ocean and stick his feet in the water just to say he'd done it once. His great-grandfather had been a sailor, or so he was told. There had been an old tintype of the man standing with a stern look and wearing a dark coat and a little dark cap perched on his head.

"He sailed to Chiny," Two Bits' mother had told him. "He'd come back with tea and yeller slaves."

"I'd like to sail to Chiny myself," Two Bits told his mother.

"It's a far ways," she said. She said the old man had gotten eaten by a whale, but Two Bits didn't believe her on that account because she was a lighthearted woman, even though she'd lived a hard live raising six kids alone, Two Bits one of the six.

Such a moon-filled night reminded Two Bits of what it must be like on the ocean, for the prairies, he reckoned, were a lot like the ocean in some ways—vast and lonesome without much to distract a feller. In the warm season, there was nothing but grass that looked like ocean waves constantly moving back and forth in the wind. Grass and sky, the same way the ocean was just water and sky. Not a spit's worth of difference he could imagine. Maybe after he killed the Mastersons, he'd take his money and Elvira and go find the real ocean and cross it and see what Chiny looked like, drink some of their tea maybe and look at yeller folks.

He saw the sign there at the edge of town—the one about NO FIRE ARMS WITHIN CITY LIMITS—and rode past it without a second glance.

He rode down Front Street looking this way and that—north of the tracks the businesses were closed. But he knew he wouldn't find a man like Bone Butcher or Bad Hand Frank, his brother-in-law—who'd sent a wire saying there was a job needed done—north of the tracks.

He crossed over the deadline, where there was noise and plenty of lights still on, and a gunshot

rang out just as he did, but he didn't think anything unusual about it. He swung in at the place
Frank said he should meet them—The Silk Garter.
Dismounted, felt stiff in the knees and hips, and
went in where it was cheery and warm, where a
crowd of drinkers and gamblers and whoremon-
gers had gathered to waste away another night.

He went to the bar and asked for Frank.

"Frank's in the jail," the barkeep said.

"Jail?"

"He shot a pimp for his blue shirt."

"Don't seem like a good enough reason to put a
feller in jail."

"The law here is hard cases," the barkeep said.
"Them damn Mastersons make it so's a feller
can't hardly enjoy life."

"So I heard. Where's the jail?"

"Back north of the tracks. You probably came
past it if you come down Front Street."

"I'm sorty looking for another feller too what's
supposed to be around here—Bone Butcher."

"Mister, you'll find him laid up in the infirmary.
Feller shot him through the foot this morning."

"Lot of shooting going on, it sounds like."

"They's a sort of madness 'round here lately, it
seems. My guess is it's the weather. Turns cold,
people get cranky. You want a drink?"

"I guess so."

"Cocktail?"

"Beer. A whiskey too."

Two Bits could almost see his shooting money

with wings on it, flying fast away, his potential employer foot shot and his brother-in-law jailed. Life was like milk: It had a way of going sour quick. Well, he'd not come all this way just to lose a job on account of people getting shot in the feet or kin tossed into jail.

"Which way to the infirmary?"

The barkeep told him how to get there, and when he arrived he saw it was just a small white structure on the east edge of town. It smelled strongly of some sort of medicine, chloroform and such, Two Bits noticed the minute he walked in the front door. He asked an orderly who was sitting in a chair eating a persimmon which of the wounded galoots was Bone Butcher.

"That big ugly one down on the end bed," the orderly said.

Two Bits clomped over and stood there at the bed, staring into a face that didn't possess a single pleasant quality. Bone's bandaged foot lay atop the blankets. "I'm Two Bits," he said. "Bad Hand Frank's brother-in-law. You said you had a job for me."

"Well, you're a talky son of a bitch, ain't you?" Bone said.

Two Bits looked around, saw that the orderly on the far side of the room was paying attention only to his persimmon.

"I dint ride all the way here to be insulted. Looks like you took one bullet already; you want another in you?"

"Ah, hell. Listen, I maybe have got more than just one job for you. You think you're up to shooting more than just those Mastersons?"

"How many others you want shot besides them?"

"Just one."

"I'll shoot as many as you want shot, for the right price."

"How much extry?"

"Do all three for five hundred each."

"That comes to around twelve hundred don't it?"

Two Bits squinted, trying to tote it. Math had been his undoing as a schoolboy, and just one more reason to quit and run off and become an assassin. You didn't need booklearning to kill folks.

"I reckon somewhere around in there, yeah," Two Bits said, thinking the figure sounded reasonable.

"Done."

"I'll need some good faith cash up front."

"How much?"

"Half."

"Half's a lot to trust to somebody I don't even know."

"You know Frank don't you?"

"Frank's in jail."

"So I heard. But you still know him. Ask him, he'll vouch for me."

"I already did, that's why you're here."

"Them's my rates, take 'em or leave 'em."

"I'll have to wait till tomorrow when I get out of here to get you the money."

"Tomorrow no later than noon, else I'm leaving." Two Bits turned to go; he didn't like the smell of medicine and the sight of shot folks. It made him think of the time he was in the army as a stretcher bearer, hauling the wounded to the surgeon's tents and seeing piles of limbs stacked up outside the tents: sawed-off legs and arms and feet. He still had dreams about piles of cut-off limbs and other bad things he'd seen.

"Don't you want to know who the extry feller is I want you to shoot?" Bone asked.

"It don't matter none to me. A feller is a feller, and a shot one is just as dead once he's shot. They all just end up stiffs."

"That's a real pleasant way of looking at it," Bone said sarcastically. "You come around my place tomorrow and I'll tell you who it is and give you the money."

Two Bits walked out and sucked in a lungful of prairie air that was cold as metal. Then he headed back down toward the deadline. Just the prospect of doing some more shooting had made him randy. He figured to take some of the forty dollars traveling money he had on him and while away the night in a most pleasant and carnal way.

He thought maybe he'd like a skinny girl this time. One that would remind him of his sweet wife, Elvira. He missed her a lot more each time he went out on a hunt.

*I guess I'm just getting old and sentimental*, he thought as he sought to find himself a nice skinny gal in a place called the Paris Club. And find one he did. He asked her her name and she said it was Mattie.

"Mattie Silks," she said.

"That's a very nice name," Two Bits said.

"You ain't nobody's feller, are you?" she said.

"Why do you ask?" Two Bits said.

"Well, I got in trouble once because I went with somebody's feller and I'd not want the same sort of trouble again."

"No, I ain't nobody's feller," Two Bits said, but feeling all the lust go out of him because of the lie he told.

"Well then, I guess it's all right," Mattie said.

Two Bits went up to her room with her and sat on the bed next to her and when Mattie began to undress Two Bits said, "It ain't necessary."

And when she said, "You in that big a hurry?"

Two Bits said, "No, it's just enough if you'll just lay down here with me."

And Mattie said, "You'd be the first feller that didn't want me to . . ."

But it was enough for him for her to be there lying next to him, Two Bits asking her to blow out the lamp's flame so the room was dark. And lying there with Mattie, Two Bits could pretend it was Elvria lying next to him and it made him feel better thinking that it was.

# *Chapter 23*

———◆———

Teddy opened his door and there they stood—Bat and Ed Masterson, and one other: Hoodoo Brown.

"'At's him," Hoodoo said, waving a long-barreled pistol.

"We need to talk," Bat said, pushing past Teddy into the room.

The Colt Lightning was there in the holster rig hanging on the back of a chair—too far to reach.

"Game's up, jailbreaker," Hoodoo said.

Bat moved between Teddy and the gun, Ed stood there in the door, blocking it.

"Man says he's a sheriff from New Mexico," Bat said. "Says you broke a prisoner out of his jail. Says the prisoner you broke out of his jail was a convicted murderer scheduled to hang. Any of this true?"

"All of it," Teddy said.

The Mastersons exchanged looks.

"Like I told you," Hoodoo Brown said. "Least the son of a bitch ain't a liar, I'll give him credit for that. I want to put the irons on him and take him back."

"Hold on," Bat said.

"For what? You heard it out of his mouth. He's a lawbreaker."

"He and I need to talk in private before anything else happens."

"Hell with that."

"You got no jurisdiction here, it's my way or no way if you want justice done."

Hoodoo Brown threw Teddy a look.

"I caught you, you lawbreaker. Nobody busts out of my jail and gets away with it. It's gone be a long ride back to New Mexico, guaranteed."

"Wait outside," Ed said, stepping forth.

Once alone with the lawmen, Bat said, "I thought you were a Pinkerton."

"I am."

"Funny sort, I'd say," Ed chimed in. "Never knew the Pinkertons to be lawbreakers."

"Least not outright lawbreakers," Bat said.

"It was a friend of mine I broke out. I don't think he got a fair trial and I wasn't just going to let them hang him."

"Very sentimental of you, but the law is still the law."

"Maybe so, but there is also something known as extenuating circumstances, and that's what I felt got overlooked in John's trial. I've got the home office working on it, trying to get him a new trial."

"Where's he at, this friend of yours? Maybe if you're willing to give him back to Sheriff Brown, I can talk him into dropping the charges against you."

"He's down in Mexico."

Bat shook his head.

"I don't know what to tell you. There's nothing I can do if I don't have a bargaining chip."

"Keep me locked up for a few days, let me send some wires to my home office. Brown can take me back down to New Mexico in a few days as easily as he can now."

"What's that going to achieve, me locking you up for a few days?"

"I don't know, maybe nothing."

Bat turned to Ed. Ed shrugged.

"It's up to you," he said.

"I guess we could wait for the circuit judge to rule on it. He'll be through in what, two, three days?"

"Friday he's scheduled in," Ed said.

"Friday then."

"That's good enough. You going to let me keep my gun?"

Bat feigned like he didn't see the humor in it, reached for the rig and handed it over to brother Ed.

Hoodoo seethed and cursed the decision when Bat informed him.

"What kind of shit thinking is that?"

Bat stopped suddenly, turned on the man. "Keep

plowing that field, my friend, and you'll get locked up too."

"Jesus H. Christ on a crutch!"

"Cool off, sheriff," Ed ordered. "You'll get your man, just not today."

"I should have brought me some deputies," Hoodoo whined.

"Maybe you should have brought a court order or a federal judge," Ed retorted.

"Go over to the Lone Star and tell the barkeep to give you a bottle of whiskey, put it on my account. For your inconvenience," Bat said. "Then go get you a room over to the Great Western, tell 'em to send me the bill."

Some of the starch went out of Hoodoo.

"Kindly of you."

"We're a friendly place when somebody gives us a chance to be."

Hoodoo looked out from under the wide brim of his dusty sombrero.

"And a mighty unfriendly one, when folks come looking for trouble," Bat added.

Hoodoo said, "Which way is it?"

"What, the saloon or the hotel?"

"Saloon. Hell, it's a drink I need, a feller can always sleep."

Bat told him how to get to the saloon, then watched him stalk off up the street like the mean, cussed son of a bitch he was.

"That's it then, walk on over to the jail with us," Bat said.

Teddy slipped on his hat and coat.

"Where we going to put him, Bat?"

"We'll double up Bad Hand Frank with the Kennedy kid."

"Frank won't like it."

"Who gives a damn what Frank likes?"

Frank didn't like it.

"Got my damn finger shot off and now you're putting me in with that snot nose," he bemoaned.

"Could put you in with them horse thieves."

Frank looked over at the three sodbusters who had stolen a string of horses from the livery. They were sallow-faced boys wearing high-water dungarees that had patches on the knees, and dirty shirts and dirty necks. Illiterate lot, one bucktoothed, one with a wandering left eye. All jugeared. Frank looked at the Kennedy kid, saw that sullen look, hated it, wanted to smack the look off the boy's face. Then he looked at the new man, the tall youthful man with the trimmed moustaches, the well-kept appearance, the one who looked like he had at least some breeding to him.

"Why not double me and him?" Frank said, pointing with his chin toward Teddy.

Ed started to say, "Frank, get your ass in one of them other cells."

But Teddy intervened, said, "It's fine with me if we bunk in together."

Bat swung the door wide and Teddy walked in and Bat closed it behind him and Ed turned the key.

"What about those messages I need to send?"

"Soon as me and Ed are through eating our breakfast, we'll come get you."

Once the brothers had left, the kid went back to sleeping under his hat. The horse thieves sat around in a tight circle mumbling to one another like dotes.

"What they put you in for?" Frank said. His hand was thickly bandaged. Some of the blood had seeped through, and where there had been white was now varying shades of pink and red.

"A misunderstanding."

Frank stood there looking out between the bars like a dog whose master had up and died on him.

"Ain't you gone ask why I'm in here?" Frank said forlornly.

"I know why," Teddy said.

"You seen it, huh?"

"Out on the street in front of the Wright House."

"It was all because of vanity. I got the goddamndest vanity of any man I ever knew and I don't even know why I'm that way."

One of the horse thieves looked back over his shoulder when Frank said the word vanity like it was the first time he'd ever heard such a word spoken. Frank returned the look; narrow-eyed and daring until the thief swung his attention back to the others.

"Then you didn't have a personal quarrel with the man you shot?" Teddy said.

"No, well, other'n he bought the shirt I wanted."

"I've heard of men dying for lots of bad reasons, but never over a shirt."

"Vanity," Frank repeated. "That's all it was."

An hour later the Mastersons returned, carrying trays of food for the prisoners. The horse thieves set upon their breakfasts like a pack of ravenous wolves. Frank picked away at his, all his appetite fled in front of the pain throbbing his hand. The kid simply rolled over and ignored his. Teddy ate like a man who had plans yet ahead of him and needed his strength to see them through.

When Teddy finished, Ed unlocked the cell door and stepped away, and Teddy went out and Ed closed and locked the door again.

"Let's take that walk," he said.

Once at the telegrapher's, Teddy wired George about the situation.

*If they take me back to Las Vegas, I might not make it back alive,* he added as his last sentence. The telegrapher looked up after reading the wire. "Send it," Teddy said.

Then Ed walked him out again and almost into the arms of Mae.

She looked first at Teddy then at Ed, said, "What have you arrested him for?"

"Let's not discuss it on the street," Teddy said.

"Where shall we discuss it, in a jail cell?"

"I'll be right over there," Ed said, nodding a

few doorways up the street. "You two got five minutes if you need 'em."

"What's going on?" Mae asked as soon as Ed walked away.

"Old problem I had before I got here."

"Did you kill somebody?"

"No, a little less dramatic than that—I broke someone out of jail that killed someone."

He saw the look in her eyes, a mixture of tenderness and confusion.

"What will they do with you?"

"There's a sheriff here who intends on taking me back to New Mexico. I'm stalling for some time. There's somebody back in Chicago that might help me out."

She started to speak, then fell silent.

"What can I do?"

"Nothing. No point in you getting mixed up in any of this."

"I want to help . . ."

"Wire a man down in Juarez, little town named Refugio. His name is John Sears. Tell him the situation. Tell him I don't expect him to come, but that he should probably move on out of that place. Mention the name Hoodoo Brown. John'll know what I mean."

She touched his hands. He looked on toward where Ed stood smoking a cheroot.

"I've got to go, Mae."

"I'll come see you later," she said.

"I wish you wouldn't."

"Can I bring you anything?"

"My razor maybe, some makings, but only if you insist on seeing me locked up."

She kissed him quickly and he turned and walked back toward where Ed was waiting.

"You ready?"

"Yeah, I'm ready, you?"

They did not see the three riders who rode into town. And the three riders didn't see them, with their eyes full of morning sun angling off those bleak prairies, and their blood full of bad whiskey.

Dirty Dave said, "Boys, this is it: Dodge, where them damn Mastersons are living, but not for long, and where the fat bank is, but will soon be empty, and where three poor bastards will soon become rich men."

Hannibal fell off his horse and Dave and Buck sat theirs looking down at him as if he were a strange object they'd suddenly come across.

"He dead?" Dave asked.

"No, he's just too drunk to ride."

"Well, it's a good thing we're where we need to be then."

Buck said, "Shit, I was hoping we could finish up here in a hurry. I miss Charlotte."

Dirty Dave started to remind him how it was him who'd said he wasn't the marrying sort, but then thought what the hell was the point—these boys were as dumb as turtles, and if it wasn't that they were such mean bastards he'd have left them back in Mister.

*I just want to kill them Mastersons,* he thought he said, but he couldn't tell if he'd actually said it or was thinking it so hard he thought he said it.

"We best find us a flop and sleep off this bad whiskey," Buck said.

## Chapter 24

———•———

The boy came one hot evening and knocked on the door, and when John opened it the boy said in Spanish, "Señor, I will pay you to teach me how to shoot this gun," and pulled from under his dirty shirt an old pistol, what John used to call a hogleg, with worn walnut grips and most of the blue rubbed off its metal.

"Why you want to fool with a thing dangerous as a rattlesnake, son?" John said.

"I need to learn to become a muchacho."

"Muchacho, eh?"

The boy took from his pockets several coins. John counted them: six pesos.

"You don't want to spend your hard-earned money on something like gun lessons," John said.

"*Si*, I do, señor."

John invited the boy inside the cooler room and out of the hot sun. John reached for the water-filled olla hanging from a peg on the wall, then reached for the olla with tequila instead and poured himself and the boy each half a cup, pushing the boy's cup across the old scarred wood blackjack table.

"A muchacho must first learn how to drink before he can go to fighting with guns," John said and took up his cup and held it forth, waiting for the boy to pick up his. Chico reached for the cup with tentative fingers, and John waited until he had it, then said, "Go on."

He watched the boy's face twist into something like displeasure at the first taste of the raw liquor, then tossed his own back and smacked his lips comically loud and said, "Let's have another."

When the boy couldn't finish his first cup John told him to come back for gun lessons when he was ready to become a true muchacho. And when the boy went outside John could hear him retching and figured it would be enough to deter him from any further thoughts of becoming a deadly gunfighting muchacho.

But the next evening the kid was back again, this time with seven pesos, and John said, "Hell, kid, you'll just get yourself blasted by some ornery cuss who won't care you're a kid, for a gun makes everyone equal and dangerous."

The boy shook his head.

John sent him off again and went the next day to see Seamus.

"He wants me to teach him how to shoot a gun, Padre."

"It is the way of young men," the priest said.

"He ain't hardly half a young man yet."

"What would you have me do, John?"

"Talk to him. I mean you're his . . ." John almost said it, the word *father* but caught himself in time. "I mean he'll respect you and listen to you maybe."

"When you were his age," the priest said, "did you listen to the advice of your elders?"

John thought back and couldn't remember a time when he was ever the age of the boy, but could remember running away from home the first time he heard a train whistle blowing off in the distance. And even though his father caught up with him eventually and brought him home again, John ran off the next year and nobody had ever caught him since.

"Why don't you satisfy his curiosity, John, and then maybe he won't be so eager to know such things," the priest said.

"Let him learn it somewheres other'n me," John said. "I don't want to be responsible in case something happens, like he takes it in his head to fight somebody with a gun over something that don't mean squat in the long run."

"But if he is taught by a professional like yourself, he'll be less likely to be foolish about guns, wouldn't you agree?"

"I thought men like you were supposed to be against such violence . . ."

"I know the truth of a boy's heart, of his wanting to become a man, and Chico has no one to teach him certain things. I know nothing at all about guns, John, or I'd teach him what it is he craves to learn. Other things I can and will teach him, but this I cannot do."

And so when the boy came again with more pesos, John finally consented to teach him how to shoot.

They went out a distance from the village, John having told Chico to gather up as many old bottles and bean cans as he could find and put them in a gunny, which the boy did.

John set the cans and bottles up, then backed the boy off twenty paces and taught him how to dry fire the pistol—an old Army Colt with the initials AJ scratched into one of the grips.

"Where'd you get this damn thing anyway?" John asked.

"I bought it from the mailman," the boy said.

"It looks like it has some history beyond that old boy," John said; Chico didn't seem to understand, but it didn't matter.

John took the boy out every day for almost a week and had him practice using the gun, holding it and cocking the hammer back and sighting down it, "like you would your finger," John said.

Chico missed about every time, so at least he didn't have to haul a new sack of bottles and cans out each evening.

"You want to aim for the biggest part of a man," John said, pointing toward his chest. "Some try head shots but they hardly ever hit anything. It's a fool's game to try and shoot a man in the head."

"Then why am I shooting at such little cans?" Chico asked wisely enough.

John looked at him as Chico ejected the spent shells. "Because if you can hit something that small, you can hit a man in his chest. Of course the thing is, them cans and bottles ain't shooting back, son. That's something you'd best keep in mind if you ever get to thinking this is an easy business. It ain't."

By the second week Chico was hitting about half the targets he aimed at, and by the third week, he was hitting most.

John watched him closely, the way he took careful aim and didn't flinch and held the gun steady, big as it was, in those small brown hands—so big he had to hold it with both hands to keep it steady.

John didn't know anything about some being natural gunfighters, like it was said of men like Hickok and others, and he couldn't say if the kid had any natural gunfighting abilities or not. Such things were only proved in the test of battle.

Finally John said, "I've taught you all I know, the rest is up to you."

Chico looked both satisfied and disappointed. "We don't come and shoot no more?"

"You're on your own, kid."

Chico handed John the pesos.

"Keep 'em, you'll need 'em for bullets for that hogleg."

The woman came often, two or three times a week, and John didn't know quite what to say to her even though he knew he looked forward to her visits and her quiet presence. He held off on any feelings as much as he could and he didn't like to guess any longer what she was feeling, and he never mentioned the note she'd left that day in his shirts and she never mentioned it either.

Sometimes he'd sit and tell her things about his life for hours on end and she never seemed to tire of listening to him. And in a way it felt like he was getting a chance to wash his soul clean by talking to her.

When she'd leave again and he'd lie there on his bunk in the dark of evenings and sometimes hear the music down in the plaza where they held the dances, he'd think of her and wonder what it would be like to dance with her and feel whole and completely human again. But he knew he could never tell her such things no matter how he wanted to at times. He could never tell her how the scent of her fresh-washed hair made him weak, or the way looking into her dark eyes made him crave to touch her.

She was the priest's woman and John still had his sin to bear, and that was simply the way it was and nothing was ever going to change that.

So on such nights, when the thirst for her became too great, John drank himself into a dark place and saw the face again and again of the woman he'd once loved and murdered in a fit of jealous rage, and not even all the tequila in Mexico could ever drown that memory.

And the boy watched the woman come and go between the haciendas of the two men.

# Chapter 25

———◆———

Hoodoo Brown's mother had warned him when he was still a boy about the evils of liquor and cards and painted women, but none of it stuck then and none of it stuck now as he drank—as they say—like a fish, trying to drown his anger over the rebuff by the Masterson brothers.

Jim cut him off after several rounds and surly talk about the weather in Kansas and the flat ugliness of the prairies and how nothing about the goddamn place was right and how only halfwits and sodbusters would find Dodge a place of charm.

"Why I never seen nothing like it," Hoodoo declared. "She's so goddamn flat and plain that if she were a woman they'd hang her for spite."

Of course little of what Hoodoo carped about made any sense to the much-enlightened Jim Masterson, except he did not like to hear his current town being run down by an outsider, a drunk and a gun toter.

"You best take your business down the line," Jim said, stoppering the bottle in front of Hoodoo that Hoodoo had been working hard at emptying and almost had.

"I was given carte blanche by your own brother," Hoodoo replied, reaching to pull the plug back out of said bottle.

But Jim placed his hand there first and said, "No sir. You done run out your carte blanche."

The two locked eyes and Jim didn't like what he saw and neither did Hoodoo Brown.

Jim could see the belly gun Hoodoo wore in his waistband, and he could feel the hickory club there under the bar with his free hand too. He was betting that if it came down to it, he could smash the club over the bastard's head quicker than the bastard could pull his gun.

"I'm the goddamn law!" said Brown.

"Not in this town you ain't."

"Law's the law no matter where."

"Tell it to the judge."

"He ain't coming till Friday."

"Tell it to him when he comes. Till then, move on down the line."

"Or what?"

"You'll soon find out what."

There was a long stringy moment of silence. Hoodoo finally gave up the idea of pulling his piece and taking life, for it was true what this particular Masterson had said about him not being the law in this particular town, and killing the brother of one who was the law would get him hanged for sure. Of all the places he'd been, Dodge was the last

place he'd want to die in. He could not imagine
having a rope slipped around his neck and looking
out and having nothing but prairies as flat as
planks in every direction as the last thing he would
ever see.

"Tell you what," says Hoodoo. "You ever get
down to Las Vegas in New Mexico, you come say
hidy and we'll finish this particular conversation
then and there. You get me?"

"I do."

"Then *adios* to you."

"Good riddance."

Hoodoo stalked out into a night filled with
snowflakes dropping out of a blood red sky the
likes of which he didn't care for; the wind
whipped the snow so it stung his face and cheeks
and eyes, and he said, "Goddamn this place and
everything in it," and went on down the walk till
he came to another saloon and went in.

His mood still foul, he ordered a beer with a
whiskey back and looked all around for a game he
could buy into, feeling a run of luck might change
his mood back again from the black that it was.

And just down from him, standing at the end of
the bar, was a singular fellow who stood under a
hat nearly as big as Hoodoo's sombrero. The fellow wore a shear coat under which he kept two
pistols that had killed lots of men, and his
thoughts were on nothing in particular except
lonesomeness. Hoodoo barely paid the fellow any
notice, this singular fellow, for he seemed no dif-

ferent than the rest, only more alone in his keeping there at the end of the bar away from everyone else.

A chair came open and Hoodoo bought into a game of five-card stud and promptly began losing some of his traveling and expense money—what the county of San Miguel called *per diem*. Eats and lodging money, in order to bring back the wanted felons he went after, in order to see that justice was served.

But the per diem money ended up in a cardsharp's pot, a man whose smooth fingers with its silver rings raked it in hand after hand while his gold-capped tooth glinted under the light.

Hoodoo folded on the tenth hand knowing he was whipped nine ways from Sunday, knowing he could not simply sit and let the slick outslick him one more time. For it was a mighty long way back to San Miguel County yet. He had tried but failed to spot something dishonest—hidden cards up the sleeve or dealing off the bottom—but if such occurred, the slick was too slick to be caught at it. It was just plain bad luck on Hoodoo's part and good luck on the sharp's.

Once more he found the bar and the sure-fire liquor and began to drink with gusto. And having counted what was left of his per diem money, Hoodoo figured there was still enough to buy himself female companionship for an hour or two and did spot a waif of a gal with pale unblemished skin—a rarity indeed—and beckoned her near with a hoot and holler.

She told him her name was Mattie Silks, was one and the same who'd brought a rare measure of comfort to the man standing singular at the bar's end—Two Bits Cline, who did take notice of the ruffian, loud and profane even when he wasn't talking. Took notice, and an immediate dislike to him.

Something rippled down through Two Bits—some form of jealousy perhaps, or maybe a fatherly instinct for children he never had; Mattie could well have been a daughter perhaps; a fair young thing who did the best she could to survive and bring men pleasure even if it meant sacrificing some of her own. To Two Bits, Mattie was a rare wildflower upon a prairie of bad grass.

Mattie came close to the oafish man from New Mexico, whose breath and person stank of sweat and liquor and lust.

Two Bits overheard the following conversation:

Hoodoo: "How much you charge, gal?"

Mattie: "It depends on what you want, mister."

Hoodoo: "I want you and all night long."

Mattie: "Ten dollars a throw, and I don't know about all night long."

It was enough to rankle Two Bits down to his boots and he moved down along the bar until he had joined the two uninvited.

A sweet smile settled on Mattie's face when she

saw the man who had been kind to her not an hour before.

"Hidy Mr. Two Bits."

"Miss Silks," Two Bits said, touching lightly the brim of his Stetson.

"Who you?" Hoodoo said.

"I'm Two Bits," Two Bits said.

"No, I mean, who you to come interfering with me and this frail sister?"

"I'm Two Bits," Two Bits said again.

" 'At don't mean shit to me."

"I'm her daddy," Two Bits said. Mattie giggled at the joke, but down deep within her bosom she enjoyed the thought that her daddy would be so gallant, for her real and true daddy had never been. In a sudden flash of memory, she remembered a man broke down in spirit and body, a man with wild hair and crazed eyes.

Hoodoo's brows wriggled like two wooly worms in a skillet.

"Say, what the hell is this!"

"She ain't for sale," Two Bits said.

Now it was Mattie's turn to look confounded.

"Then what is she, winder dressing?"

Hoodoo grabbed Mattie hard by the wrists with it in mind to haul her upstairs where the cribs were. Such he'd noticed earlier, each crib marked by a red curtain, and further, he'd seen this same skinny gal taking up a customer or two herself, so it was with great chagrin he was being interfered with by what looked like a crusty old man.

But when Hoodoo made his move, Two Bits made his: swept off his hat and slapped Hoodoo two or three fast times across the face with it, then plopped it back on his head just as quick.

It took a full second for the insult to spark in Hoodoo's besotted brain, but when it did, the insult grew from a tiny flame to a raging fire.

Hoodoo reached for his belly gun and Two Bits reached for his own trusty pistols.

And *Bang! Bang! Bang!*

Shots were fired.

Hoodoo fell back with his shirt ablaze and two holes in him spilling blood. He fell grasping and clawing the air and somebody took a spittoon and tossed its putrid contents on him to douse the flame as he squirmed on the dirty floor, where men had stood and spat and missed, staining the floorboards for several years. And as he lay dying, Hoodoo recalled the warnings and admonitions of his dear sweet ma about the evils of liquor and cards and painted women and knew she'd been right all along.

It was too late now and maybe he'd see her on the other side.

He felt the prairie wind and the snow falling from a blood red sky into his very bones as the world and all that was in it seemed to slip as quietly away as a burglar—a thief who was taking with him Hoodoo's very soul.

Then the lovely young face leaned in close and he could see that Mattie Silks had different col-

ored eyes—one green, one brown—and he wondered why he ever chose her in the first place.

"Oh faithless child," he uttered.

She didn't know what he meant and neither did
Two Bits Cline, whose guns were still leaking
smoke.

Two little lead pills was all that struck Hoodoo
down, but it felt like there was an elephant standing on his chest and that it wasn't ever going to
get off.

His glassy gaze shifted from Mattie to Two Bits.

"You . . . you . . ." he said.

"It sure was," Two Bits said.

Now above him a whole circle of faces had
gathered and joined those of Two Bits Cline and
Mattie Silks. Then there appeared among the
faces two he recognized: the Masterons, Bat and
Ed. It felt suddenly as though he were falling
down a well and the world got dark and cold and
awfully lonely.

Of course the law wanted to know who he was
and what happened and several replies were
forthcoming, most defending the actions of Two
Bits, the little stranger in the big hat who came to
the cyprian's aid having seen, they said, the way
the now dead man had assaulted her by grabbing
her roughly. They were in accordance on the facts.

"Self-defense," they shouted.

But Bat then asked a very pointed and legal
question.

"Didn't you see the sign at the city limits about no firearms?"

"I can't read," Two Bits said.

"Ignorance is no excuse to break the law," Ed said.

"I ain't never had nobody call me ignorant before."

"You best give up them guns or clear out of town, mister," Bat said. "That's a lawman you shot there."

"Well then, you'd think he'd know it was wrong to assault a woman."

Bat and Ed traded looks. "What's it to be, turn in your guns or leave town?" Bat said.

"I'll leave. It don't seem like a friendly place whatsoever."

"You make sure you do. We catch you around here wearing pistols again, we'll lock you up and toss away the key."

"You the Mastersons I heard so much about?"

"We are and what about it?"

Two Bits felt like his luck was unfolding just about right.

# Chapter 26

---

Bat unlocked the cell.

"You're free to go."

"How come?" Teddy asked.

"That sheriff from New Mexico, Brown, he got himself killed last night."

"You don't want to hold me till they can send someone else?"

"Hell no. Whatever their problems are in New Mexico, aren't mine or Ed's."

"Much obliged."

"What about me?" Bad Hand Frank said.

"What about you?"

"You could let me go too, I'd leave town."

"Right," Bat said, closing the door shut again and locking it.

Bat walked out to the front part of the jail, where Ed's office was. He opened a desk drawer and took out Teddy's gun rig.

"You sure about this, Sheriff?"

"I am."

"Then I'll get back to work."

"It might be better if you moved on. Some other

lawman might just show up from New Mexico once they get word their man is dead."

"I figure if they do send someone it will be at least a week before he arrives. That should give me time to finish the job I came here for."

"Suit yourself. But just remember, a bird only gets so many chances to fly."

"I'll keep that in mind."


Teddy walked to the Wright House and went in. Mae almost dropped a tray of food when she saw him. Instead she served it to a table of business types, men in stripped suits and paper collars, then hurried over.

"How did you—"

"It looks like you're busy. Why don't I explain later?"

"You didn't—"

"No, they let me go." He could see the relief on her face and it made him feel good that she cared so much.

"Coffee, something to eat?"

"Yes, both."

She took his order and hurried off and came back twenty minutes later with his meal. "I've arranged to get off early," she said.

"Great."

"We need to talk."

He heard the urgency in her voice. "Yeah, I might not be able to stay in Dodge too much longer, the way things are going."

"I sent the wire to your friend, by the way."

"Good."

"I have to get back to waiting the tables. Come pick me up at noon if you can, otherwise I'll wait for you at the boarding house."

He nodded and they exchanged looks, and he watched her as she went off to wait on another table. He ate quickly and left.

He needed to check out Angus Bush. Process of elimination, he told himself. If it wasn't Bush, then that brought it down to Bone Butcher, according to Dog Kelly at least. He crossed the street and started down to the deadline. He decided to make a brief stop at Dog's Alhambra saloon to see if anything further had developed.

He noticed Ed and Bat standing out front of Ed's office, talking.

Then he saw something that put him on alert: three men coming up the street from a direction behind the Mastersons. Normally he wouldn't have thought twice about it, but he knew by the way the men were moving—the way they were armed with their coats thrown open to show the pistols punched into their waistbands, and one of them carrying a shotgun—that they weren't out for a morning stroll. They looked rough in their dirty slouch hats and dusty long coats. They were trouble all the way around and they were headed straight toward the Mastersons, who hadn't yet noticed them.

He went quickly toward where Bat and Ed stood talking, hoping his movement wouldn't alert the three shootists too soon. He saw them fan out, two of them stepping into the street, the one with the shotgun bringing it up to his shoulder.

Teddy was ten yards from the brothers.

"Bat!" he yelled, breaking into a dead run, drawing the Lightning from his shoulder rig.

Bat looked up first, his face full of uncertainty.

Teddy didn't wait to explain, but took aim at the shotgunner and fired. The bullet missed, but it was enough to alert the Mastersons they were under attack. They both turned, drawing their weapons, and as they did the air suddenly crackled with the sound of pistol fire and the big boom of the shotgun, whose pellets shattered the windows of Ed's office.

Teddy stopped running and brought his gun to bear on the man with the sawed-off, who was breaking it open now to plug in a new set of shells. The gunfighter's calm took over as Teddy took careful aim, and he could see the brothers coolly standing their ground, firing as well. But even the coolest head under withering gunfire could miss an otherwise easy target.

The man with the shotgun snapped it shut again and brought it up, taking aim at Bat, who was busy returning the fire of the other two, who had taken refuge—one behind a wagon and the other behind a porch post.

*One shot,* Teddy's instinct told him. *One shot or he kills Bat.*

It was a distance of some forty paces, he figured. The odds were long that he could drop the man at such a distance with a handgun, but the odds didn't really play into it as he brought the front blade sight down on the man's upper torso and fired.

The Lightning kicked in his hand. The bullet spun the shotgunner sideways. He cried out, dropping the sawed-off, but then steadied himself and bent to pick it up again.

Bat turned in time to see the action just as Ed got hit and went down.

Bat flashed a quick look at Teddy, but Teddy was already drawing bead on the man again, and when the shotgunner's hands reached the stock of the double-barrel, Teddy pulled the trigger.

They'd put together a hasty plan. Well, Dirty Dave had put together the plan and Buck and Hannibal had gone along with it.

Dave had said, "We'll wait for 'em to come out on the street first thing, and when they do, we'll walk up on 'em and shoot 'em before they get the sleep out of their eyes."

"Risky," Hannibal said.

"Everything is," Dave said. "Soon's we shoot 'em, we'll walk straight over and rob that bank and be rich men."

"We could get shot," Buck said. "I thought we was going to shoot 'em in their sleep."

"We can't wait to catch 'em sleeping. We might get one but not the other. No, boys, the longer we wait the riskier it is—the element of surprise, that's the trick. I've thought this thing through and I think we'll just surprise 'em, and today's as good a day as any."

Still, Hannibal and Buck were somewhat reluctant, but Dave had made up a story for them: He told them he'd heard the bank was flush with money and that a big payroll was being shipped out that very day on the noon flyer.

"We don't do this today, half the money will be gone from that bank."

"We could rob the dang train," Buck said.

"Remember what I told you about what happened to Jake Crowfoot? I ain't about to rob no dang train and fall under its wheels and be cut to ribbons, you?"

And so it was agreed that they'd wait on the street that early morning until the two brothers could be spotted and then take action.

It happened like Dave had predicted it would and the brothers appeared in front of the jail together and Dave said, "Let's go shoot them sons a bitches," and Buck said, "Why not?"

"Yeah, why the hell not?" Hannibal said. Hannibal was carrying a shotgun. "I can do some mean work with this."

"You sure as hell can," Buck said and grinned

and felt happy with the two pistols stuck inside his belt because he'd soon be a rich man.

It was Dirty Dave who saw the stranger running their direction as they approached the Mastersons.

"Who the fuck is that?"

The boys offered blank looks.

"Deputy maybe?" Buck said.

"Possible," Dave said. "Kill him too. You boys fan out."

Hannibal felt the bullet hit him and it was like a punch that caused his arms to go momentarily numb and spun him around. He'd been shot before, but not this bad, he told himself. Instinct made him bend to pick the shotgun up again. But when he touched it, the world as he knew it disappeared.

Teddy turned his attention to the other two, saw one go down, figured Bat had shot the man, since Ed himself was down and struggling to get up again. Teddy fired on the remaining man, so did Bat. Both shots hit Dirty Dave almost at the same instant.

Dave felt air under his boots, felt himself being lifted and it was a sort of pleasant feeling for a moment. Then he was slammed to the ground and he had a hard time breathing.

*Why am I chewing this goddamn dirt?* he wondered. It was a gritty terrible taste as the pain of something white-hot crawled through his blood, seemed to clutch at his heart and squeeze, caused him to chew the ground he lay facedown on. He turned his head and spat. That is when he saw the quizzical stare of Buck Pierce, those colorless eyes looking at him as if to say What the hell happened to us? Dave saw too, some of Buck's jaw had been shot off—a piece of white bone in a red glistening maw of raw meat where the chin should have been.

Bat turned to help Ed to his feet, saw that he was shot through the lower portion of his leg. Teddy walked down the street toward the fallen men, gun cocked and aimed, knowing that dead men weren't always as dead as they seemed.

"You hit?" Bat shouted.

"No. How's Ed?"

"He'll live."

Teddy stood over the shotgunner. His second shot had ripped through the man's skull ear to ear. There was no life in him.

He moved on to the other two, saw that one had half his face shot away. The other was still breathing but his wounds were grievous.

Bat sat Ed in a chair there in front of the jail and came over and stood next to Teddy.

Bat shook his head, said, "Goddamn Dave, I guess you won't be escaping any more mud jails."

"You know this one?" Teddy said.

"Dirty Dave Rudabaugh. Me and Ed have been chasing his ass almost as long as we've been the law."

"Well, it looks like you won't have to chase him anymore."

"Looks like it."

In spite of his wounds Dave was gasping. "Water . . . oh, Lord, I need water."

By now the streets were crowded with locals who'd come to see what the commotion was about. They moved in close to the dead and the living.

Bat looked at some of the men and said, "Well, take this one to Doc's. I doubt he'll live, but I won't have him lying here like a run-over dog. Some of you boys take them other two over the undertaker and see he gets 'em buried. Tell him it's to be a plain and nothing fancy burying since the county's paying."

"What about Ed?" one of them said.

"Hell, I almost forgot. Take him to Doc's too."

Once the dead and wounded had been removed, the streets cleared of spectators.

Bat said, "I need to go check on Ed, but . . ."

"You don't need to say it," Teddy replied.

"Yeah, I do. I owe you, and I apologize for being such a damn stick about you coming here. That was a damn fine piece of shooting, Mr. Blue."

"Damn fine piece of shooting to you too, Bat."

Bat let a half smile cross his mouth, then held out his hand and Teddy shook it.

Dog Kelly had been among the many who came to see the aftermath of the shootout.

"They's blood on the streets of Dodge again, but thank God it ain't none of yours or the Masterson brothers. You think them's the ones hired to kill 'em?"

"That would be my guess."

"Mine too."

"I guess I just need to find out now who it was hired 'em."

"I guess."

"I was on my way over to Angus Bush's place when this broke out."

"Just heard, for your information, that Bone Butcher got out of the infirmary a while ago. You best keep an eye on him, he might be gunning for you, since you shot him in the foot."

"I doubt he wants any more of me, but if so he can have what he thinks he can handle."

"Just so's you know," Dog said.

"I've been informed."

Dog Kelly still looked snake bit with sadness: He had a handful of silk flowers he had been taking to Dora's grave when he heard the shooting.

"Thought she might appreciate 'em," Dog said almost self-consciously when he saw Teddy had taken notice of them.

"I'm sure she will."

Teddy watched Dog go off toward the cemetery looking like a sad little man who would never find happiness again. He walked past the bloodstains in the street and kept going.

# *Chapter 27*

———◆———

A ngus Bush stood behind the bar, the dim light
long in the room as it fell through the narrow
doors. The club was empty that time of day. Angus had a newspaper spread in front of him on the hardwood, a mug of coffee next to it. He looked up when Teddy walked in, then glanced again at his newspaper.

"You got any more of that coffee?" Teddy said.

"Sure."

Teddy waited until Angus poured him a cup.

"I'm leaving town in a day or so," Teddy said.

Angus shrugged, said, "That supposed to mean something to me?"

"Only if you remember my offer from when I first came in and want to take advantage of my services before I go."

Angus looked up.

"What makes you think I need to hire a gun?"

Teddy blew steam off the coffee. "Nothing makes me think it, I'm just offering if you have a need."

"I don't."

"You sure?"

Angus placed both beefy fists atop the newspaper. "I need anyone killed, I reckon I could do the job myself. But the fact is, I don't need anybody killed. I'm a contented man. I got me a nice little business and I make a little bit of money at it and that's enough. I saw enough killing in the war to last me a lifetime. That answer your question, mister?"

"It does."

"I heard gunshots earlier, you know anything about that?"

Teddy shook his head, said no. He felt no need to discuss it with Angus Bush.

"Someday they'll tame this town," Bush said. It will be sweet music to my dear ears when they don't hear another gunshot or cuss word. Don't know why a man can't just come into my place and buy himself a drink and play a little cards without all the other that tends to go with it. What's wrong with that?"

"Nothing," Teddy said.

Angus nodded, went back to reading his newspaper.

"How much for the coffee?" Teddy said.

"It's on the house, call it a farewell drink," Angus said.

Teddy knew he had eliminated one of the suspects.

He felt drained but knew he had to go on. A lot

had happened over the last twenty-four hours, none of it good. The only saving grace had been Mae. He remembered her saying how they needed to talk, that there was something she needed to tell him. He was prepared for the worst, that she had decided to leave Dodge, and that they would probably never see each other again.

Well, disappointment seemed to come in spades in a town like Dodge, and he guessed he ought to be prepared for anything at this point. He swung by the infirmary on his way to see Mae to check on Ed Masterson.

Ed was lying on a narrow bed with his leg bandaged and propped up on a pair of pillows. Bat sat next to the bed, shifting his derby in his fidgeting hands.

"Looks like you might have saved me and Bat's bacon, you coming along when you did," Ed said. His brow was beaded with sweat. A wood burner stood in the corner; flames flickered behind the isinglass in the small door. The room was hot and stuffy, full of the odor of sickness and medicinal liniments.

"Pure luck that I came along when I did," Teddy said.

"Maybe the coming-along part, but not the shooting part."

Bat interjected, "This feller is full of surprises, Brother Ed. Next thing we know, he'll be performing rope tricks."

"I know it," Ed said.

Both brothers grinned. Teddy wasn't sure if he should. "How's the leg?"

"Bullet went clean through. Hell, I don't even know why I'm laying here instead of doing my rounds."

Teddy glanced toward the opposite end of the room, where Dirty Dave Rudabaugh lay, his eyes closed, his skin pasty. "What about him?"

"Doc says he should up and die any minute, but he ain't dead yet, and I got the worst feeling he ain't going to either. Dirty Dave's got the god-damnedest luck I ever seen a man have. Shot twice and he still ain't dead." Bat's expression was one of chagrin.

"I just spoke to Angus Bush. You can cross him off your list," Teddy said.

"How can you be sure?" Bat asked.

"I'm sure."

Bat looked at Ed and Ed shrugged, said, "I reckon he's been right on most things so far, I ain't one to quarrel with him on this."

"Neither am I," said Bat. "Consider Angus crossed off the list."

"Dog figures that leaves Bone Butcher."

"I don't know how I'll get it out of him, unless I beat it out of him," Bat said. "Which is something I'm not opposed to doing."

"He might shake loose out of this town once he hears the men he hired failed their task," Teddy said.

"He might. And if he doesn't, I'll give him twenty-four hours to get out," Bat said. "That is, if he doesn't confess first. If he does, I might just put a bullet in him and save the county a trial."

"You don't want to do that."

"Hell, I don't see why not."

"Well, I guess that's it then," Teddy said. "I'll stick around till you question Bone, but I reckon my work here is pretty much finished."

"I reckon so. Once word gets out that assassinations of the local law get you an early grave, it might stop others who think it's a way to easy money."

"We can only hope," Ed said.

Ed held forth his hand. "Mr. Blue. I owe you. We both do."

"No. Let's just call it even."

"How soon you heading out?" Bat said.

"Day or two."

"Stop by the office before you go."

Teddy nodded, shook Ed's hand. The hand felt warm, feverishly warm, but still with a good grip to it.

"I'll see you boys later."

The weather had cleared, but the streets were still muddy from the previous snowfall now melted away mostly. Sun sparkled in the puddles left behind, making them look like shattered glass lying in the street. The air was clean, and at least there wasn't the smell of gunsmoke in it and that was something to be said.

Teddy passed the undertaker's. Both the newly dead men—Hannibal Smith and Buck Pierce—were propped up in the window, their arms and legs bound with wire and tied to boards. Hand-printed signs around their necks read: THE WAGES OF SIN. For added effect, the mortician had propped Hannibal's empty shotgun in his arms. The dead men had sleepy expressions, like they were having bad dreams they couldn't quite awaken from.

*Jesus Christ!* Teddy thought.

Teddy found Mae waiting for him at the Wright House. She was sitting at a table by herself.

"Should we talk here, or go elsewhere?" he said.

"Is the cab still available for rent?"

"Sure. I'll go get it."

"I'll walk with you."

They went to the livery and rented the cab and Mae said, "Let's go to that spot where we had the picnic." They sky had almost cleared completely of clouds and an unusually warm southerly wind blew gentle compared to the previous cold. Teddy popped the reins and set the horse into a trot, he felt anxious and wanted to get the talking started. Mae fell silent beside him, her eyes darting over the plains of withered grass.

Soon enough they arrived at the spot where they'd gone the first time. Teddy helped her from the cab then ground-reined the horse. Mae stood facing into the wind, for several long moments her eyes closed.

"There's something I need to tell you," Teddy said.

She pursed her lips.

"I had to kill a man today, possibly two if the other one dies."

He saw her face tighten.

"It couldn't be helped, they were going to assassinate the Mastersons. It just happened that I was there."

She opened her eyes and stared at him.

"There's something else, too. I'm a Pinkerton detective. It's why I came here in the first place, to prevent the Mastersons from getting assassinated."

"I heard about the shooting," she said. "I fretted that you'd been hurt. I can't tell you how relieved I was when I saw you come in."

He saw her lips tremble, thought it was over worry for him. He put his arms around her, said, "As you can see, I'm all right, Mae."

"It isn't that."

"What is it then?"

"Can I ask you something first?"

"Yes," he said.

"How does it make you feel, to have had to kill someone?"

"Like hell," he said. "Even though it couldn't be helped, it doesn't make me feel any better about it." He didn't want to tell her the rest of what he felt, the fact that the killing got easier. He didn't know how to explain that part. How the first man he'd killed had left him feeling physically ill, but not the second nor the third. And while he didn't like to think about taking another man's life, he knew now he would not lose any sleep over it like he had the first one. It bothered him that he'd become that way more than the actual shootings.

"How ironic," she said, her voice fading with the wind. "Now there is something I have to tell you."

Teddy saw the serious look in her eyes, knew that whatever it was she was about to tell him couldn't be good news.

"Go ahead."

The winds shifted and suddenly she felt chilled and said, "Do you mind if we sit in the cab out of this?"

He helped her step into the cab, then went around and took the reins and got in next to her.

"I'm listening."

"I don't know quite where to begin," she said. "Suffice it to say that you and I have a connection."

"I know that already."

"No, I don't think you understand. The connection we have goes back several years."

"You're right, I don't understand."

"I'm not from Canada like I said. I wasn't married to a man who brought me here."

The horse took a sudden step and the cab

lurched forward and Teddy pulled back on the reins.

"Say it plainly, Mae."

"It was my brother who killed your brother," she said.

At first the words didn't want to register right. It seemed too impossible what she was telling him.

"My name is Mae Carnahan," she said. "My brother was Ludlow Carnahan."

Teddy felt stunned. "No," he said.

"Yes. It's true. I wanted to tell you ever since we first met and you told me your name, but I couldn't be sure that there was any connection— that your last name wasn't simply a coincidence, so I sent some inquires back to Chicago and learned that you were really Horace's brother."

He felt a knot in his chest.

"And when it was confirmed who you were, I struggled whether to tell you at all who I was. I'd already begun to fall in love with you . . . and I didn't want to lose you by admitting the awful truth."

"What is the truth, Mae? I mean, what the hell is the truth?"

"I know you're angry," she said. "You've every right to be."

He climbed down from the cab. He had to breathe; it felt like he couldn't. He walked off a distance, his mind full of confusion, regret, anger.

She came after him.

"Teddy, it was a horrible and tragic thing that

happened to Horace and I don't blame you if you hate me now for telling you the truth, but I came to realize that if I didn't, we could never have anything real between us. I'm telling you now out of the same love that kept me from telling you sooner."

He turned on her, trying hard to keep his anger from spilling over.

"Tell me why he did it!"

"He did it for me."

"I don't understand that sort of reasoning."

"Horace was in love with me, Lud found out. Lud was jealous and—"

"It happened in a . . ."

"I know where it happened," she said. "I worked there. Horace was determined to take me out of that place, to make an honest woman of me. And I . . . I was prepared to let him."

"You said your brother was jealous of you . . ."

"Yes, he loved me, in his own sick way he loved me in the way that any man loves a woman."

"And what about you?"

"No. I could never do anything like that. It seemed to make Lud all the more insane with jealousy because I wouldn't return his love. Maybe if I had, he might not have murdered Horace. I've asked myself over and over again if there was anything I could have done to have prevented it . . ."

"My sources told me the woman's name was Desiree Drake."

"It was the name I used to protect who I really

was. Lud said it sounded more sophisticated, more like the name of a whore. But Mae is my real name and I took it back after Lud died."

"I still can't believe any of this," Teddy said. Then he remembered what else was in her file that George had shown him the day he recruited Teddy to be an operative for the Pinkertons: a strawberry birthmark in the shape of a star on her left hip—this Desiree Drake. He hadn't seen such on Mae and said as much.

"You've never seen me naked in the light," she said.

And now that he thought about it, he hadn't.

"Show me," he said.

She did. And when she did, it made it true and it brought the mystery and that chapter of his life to a close. And they stayed out there like that, talking the rest of the afternoon until the sun went down behind them and darkness crawled once more upon the land.

And finally he said, "I don't know what I'm feeling towards you, Mae. I don't know what I should feel."

"I understand that you don't," she said. "Take me back and you think about it and when you've decided how you feel, come and tell me, either way. You owe me at least that much."

And he nodded and helped her into the cab and they drove back through the gloaming, the feeling of a knife twisting in his heart.

# Chapter 28

———•◆•———

Dusk descended like a cloud of fret. Two Bits had kept out of sight knowing that if the Mastersons spotted him they'd arrest him or he'd have to kill them, and he wasn't about to kill them for free, when Bone Butcher was offering him a thousand dollars and maybe more, because Bone said there was another he wanted killed too.

When the last light of day winked out and the lights of the saloons south of the deadline came on, Two Bits made his way up and down alleys until he came to the back door of the Silk Garter and entered unnoticed.

He found Bone in his office, his shot foot propped atop a fancy footstool with a yellow silk pillow with fringes.

"I come to seal the bargain," Two Bits said.

" 'Bout time you come here, I thought you said you was leaving town by noon it we didn't make some sort of an agreement."

"Things happened," Two Bits said. "Unexpected things not in my control that put the kibosh on my plans. But I'm here now and I'm ready to collect my money and see the job done."

"So I heard about them unexpected things. Word is you killed a lawman from New Mexico."

"Word travels fast."

"Who paid you to kill him?"

"Nobody."

"You killed him for free?"

"I guess you could look at it that way."

"Then I oughter get a discount on them Mastersons."

"I almost killed 'em free too, and I might kill you free if you don't stick to the deal we had. Hell, I might kill everybody in this dang town—it ain't the friendliest place I ever been."

Bone Butcher could see the impatience in the little feller's eyes.

"No, no, we still got us a deal. Thing is, I need me yet another feller killed on top of the three I already mentioned." Bone was thinking hard about Frenchy stealing the Rose from him.

"It don't make no difference to me how many you want killed. Only question is, how much you willing to pay for all these extra fellers?"

"I figure four fellers deserves a discount, don't you?"

Two Bits was down to lint in his pockets, having spent most everything he had on Mattie Silks and liquor. If he had been flush, he'd have told the foot-shot feller to kiss his mangy ass, that he wasn't giving no discounts no how and no way.

But as it stood, if he was ever going to take Elvira and go see the ocean, he'd need to earn as much quick cash as he could.

"All right," he said. "How much a discount?"

"Say fifteen hundred for all four, 'at comes out to about eight hundred apiece."

Two Bits tried to tote the figure in his head knowing he had to divide one figure into the other, but the math eluded him as Bone Butcher knew that it would.

"Done. But I need a down payment."

"Why?"

Two Bits looked at him hard from under that big hat. "You take me for an idjit?"

"Okay, how about a third now and the rest when it's finished?"

"How much would a third come to?"

"Three hundred? A third is three, that's why they call it a third."

"Then hand it over and tell me who them other two is you want shot."

Bone had given some thought to killing all three Masterson brothers but figured if Ed and Bat bit the bullet, Jim would hightail it out of town, being the most fey of the trio, and thus save Bone some on the killings. Bone also planned a little surprise for Two Bits too, when he came to claim the rest of his money—the surprise being the derringer there in the safe next to his considerable sums of money from which he counted out the three hundred. Why, the town would see him as some sort of hero for killing the man who assassinated the Mastersons. They'd probably elect him city marshal—now wouldn't that be choice, he thought.

"Them other two besides the Mastersons," Bone said. "One is named Frenchy LeBreck—he runs the Paris Club, not far from here. Little prissy feller with thin moustaches. The fourth one I want dead is the son of a bitch that shot my toes off and is the one Frenchy hired to kill me, a lanky cuss name of Teddy Blue."

"Looks like you was lucky he only shot your toes off," Two Bits said, stuffing the cash into his pocket.

"Lucky my ass. You ever had your toes shot off?"

"Can't says I have and can't says I'm planning to. Where will I find this yahoo?"

"I asked around, he's staying at the Dodge House, room twelve, top of the stairs."

"Twelve sounds like an unlucky number. Least it will be when I finish with him."

"Was me, I'd start by killing the easy ones first."

"I don't need you to tell me my job. They'll all be dead by morning."

"Good, good, and when they are, come see me and I'll give you the rest of your cash."

"You can count on it, bub."

Two Bits slipped out as he'd slipped in, through the back door and down alleys until he found the Paris Club.

He ambled to the bar and asked for Frenchy.

"He's back in his room," the barkeep said.

"It's important I talk to him. I got some money for him," Two Bits said, pulling out the fold of cash. "Three hundred dollars, I owe him. I know he wants it bad."

The barkeep whistled.

"Back down that hall," he said, pointing with his eyes.

Two Bits took the journey slow, walking on cat's feet. The noise from the main room seemed to follow him. He came to a door and could see a light spilling from underneath it a few inches into the hall. He put his ear to the door and listened. He couldn't hear anything. He pulled out one of his pistols and turned the knob and it gave way. He opened the door suddenly and stepped in, closing it quietly behind him. There in the middle of the room was a big copper tub full of water. Candles were lit and flickering all over the room, their little lights dancing along the walls. It felt spooky to Two Bits, the way the shadow and light intermingled, and it raised the hair on the back of his neck. He listened hard. Then he heard some sounds coming from up in a loft there the other side of the room, where a little set of steps led to.

Two Bits figured maybe Frenchy was up there asleep and the sounds he heard were snores. He didn't favor shooting nobody in their sleep—it seemed cowardly somehow to kill a sleeping man. But these were desperate times and if he had to, he'd shake the feller awake then shoot him. He moved to the foot of the steps. Then he heard voices. The voices were saying little love things.

"You are my little sad dove," a man's voice said.

"I have broken my wing and you have taken me in," a woman's voice said.

"I am your refuge," the man's voice said.

"I am your little sad dove," the woman's voice said.

"I can't believe my good luck, having the Rose of Cimarron in my bed."

"That's all well and good," Two Bits said soon as he mounted the stairs and saw two people lying on a small cot together. One of them had moustaches and he looked prissy.

"You must be Frenchy."

"*Oui*," Frenchy said. "That is who I am, who are you?"

"Mr. Butcher sent me."

He saw then the looks on their faces and felt sorry for them and said, "Maybe it would be better if you closed your eyes," then took a pillow and shot them through it. A spew of feathers fluttered in the air like tiny doves, then drifted downward. Just two quick shots and it was finished.

"Boy, oh, boy. I sure am beginning to hate this line of work," Two Bits said to himself looking at the woman and then gently closing her eyes because she seemed to be staring straight up at him.

She was the first woman he ever had to shoot. It upset his stomach some.

There was a bottle of wine next to the cot and Two Bits took a long swallow from it, then another. It wasn't sweet like he heard wine was supposed to be. Almost tenderly he covered the two lovers with the quilt, then slipped out again.

Now he needed to find either the Mastersons or the one called Teddy Blue. Two Bits had a good memory for names. He decided to shoot this Blue feller first, since shooting one man was a bit easier than shooting two—especially two like the Mastersons. He slipped quietly out the back door of the Paris Club and into the night just moments before Leo, Frenchy's number-one bartender, brought the tray of food Frenchy had ordered earlier to the back room. The tray contained oysters on the half shell, various cheeses, and a nice bottle of champagne. Frenchy had it in mind to propose marriage to the Rose of Cimarron. He'd bought a small silver ring with a garnet he was going to present right after they'd feasted.

Leo knocked politely on Frenchy's door. No answer. He knocked again. No answer. He tried the knob and the door opened without protest. He saw the many candles flickering, the tub. He touched his fingers to the water and the water was cool.

"Frenchy," he called up toward the loft. No answer. Maybe they had fallen asleep, Frenchy and the lovely Rose.

The tray clattered all the way down the steps when Leo climbed them and looked at the quilt-covered lumps on the bed and saw the big bloody wet stains.

Bat Masterson had just finished his brother's rounds north of the deadline and was about to head south of it before retiring for the evening. He had in mind a few hands of poker and a big steak before going over to see Bone Butcher. He wanted to feel good and relaxed before he started beating a confession of conspiracy out of him. He had a head full of ideas of how he'd get Bone to talk; shooting him in the same foot Teddy had shot him in was one of the options Bat considered. He rather relished the idea.

But then he saw Leo running up the street still wearing his apron, shouting, "Sheriff, Sheriff!"

"Who did this?" Bat said, after viewing the bodies. There were bloody feathers and a shot pillow scattered on the floor.

Leo shrugged.

"You didn't hear a gunshot?"

"It's loud out in the main room."

"He was smart, whoever he was. He shot 'em through the pillow to muffle the sound. It's that goddamn . . ." Bat started to say the name Bone Butcher, but thought better of it. He didn't want a lynching, and he couldn't be a hundred percent positive it was Bone's hand in it. Besides, Bone was laid up with a shot foot and wouldn't have done this dreadful thing himself. So it would have had to been someone Bone sent to do the dirty work. And that thought led to another darker thought, one that sent a little chill through him. If this was Bone's doing, if he had hired someone to kill Frenchy and the Rose, then it was real possible that the same person had been hired to kill him and Ed as well.

*Jesus.* Could there be more than that trio of morons Dirty Dave put together to assassinate him and Ed? And with Ed laid up, it would be just him alone to face whoever was out there. Unless . . .

He went to find Teddy Blue.

# Chapter 29

She came again that night and knocked on his door and when John opened it and saw her standing there, he wasn't surprised and he wasn't unhappy about it, but he wasn't pleased either.

He looked beyond her into the dark brown dusk and didn't see the priest out there as he had on other occasions.

She had a bowl of fruit she held forth to him like a gift.

"You shouldn't have come," he said.

Her large dark eyes searched his face.

He stepped away from the door and she wedged herself into the room as though she were shy or as though he might strike her, and set the bowl of fruit on the small table, one of the two pieces of furniture in the room—the other being the small bed in the corner.

"Thank you for the fruit," he said.

She looked at him, her eyes full of questions that she could not ask because she was a mute.

"You probably should go," John said. "Seamus will be waiting for you."

She shook her head and her thick black rope of hair seemed to him like a thing he wanted to touch but he'd refrained so far and would now.

"Look, Selena," he said. "If it were other than what it is between you and him, I'd take up with you in a heartbeat. But you belong to him and I respect that and I won't come between the two of you. And if he does leave and doesn't take you with him, you're free to come live here with me. But I just can't be part of . . ."

She came to him and laid her head on his chest and put her arms around him, and she was like a sad little child who needed to be held and he could not refuse.

She felt warm and slight to him like a child. They stayed that way for a time but then he eased her away.

"You must go back," he said.

She mouthed the question: "Why?"

"Because I know what it is like to be on the other side of something like this. I know what it is Seamus must feel, knowing that you come here to visit me. I've been in his shoes and the outcome wasn't very pleasant."

She didn't understand, of course, and he didn't feel like going through the whole story over again with her about his having shot the woman he'd been in love with, the one he'd caught with another man.

And the reminder of that tragedy was fresh in

his mind, since the telegram had arrived this noon warning him that Hoodoo Brown had come to Dodge and had Teddy arrested and that John ought to get into the wind and find another place to lay low.

His first thought had been to go north and help his old amigo out of his jam. But, he rightly reasoned, by the time he got to Dodge, Hoodoo would have hauled Teddy back to Las Vegas—or worse—a thought he didn't want to contemplate—killed him on the trail and left him buried in an unmarked grave.

John figured to go north anyway, not to Dodge, but to Las Vegas, and await Hoodoo's arrival back in that town with or without Teddy Blue. And one way or the other, he'd either save Teddy's hide or kill Hoodoo Brown. That was John's fate as he saw it, but the constant visits from the mute woman were complicating matters more than he wanted.

She looked at him now with a great sadness that he would not accept her. She took a piece of paper and wrote something on it and handed it to him and he had to bend down to the lamplight to read it, for his eyes were failing him.

*Is it because I can't talk that you don't want me?*

"No," he said. "No, Selena. It don't have anything to do with it. You're beautiful and any man would want you. But there is already one man who loves you."

She wrote again.

*He is going to leave me and go north.*

John read it, straightened and said, "When that day comes, I'll be waiting here for you."

She mouthed silent words he could not understand.

"There's something I need to tell you," he said. "I have to go north for a time myself, but I aim on coming back soon as I finish up some business there."

He saw then that she didn't believe him. She wrote:

*You are leaving me too.*

He tried to tell her that wasn't the case, but she ran out, tears streaming down her cheeks. He stood in the door watching until the night took her. She ran toward the church, and at least that was some comfort for him.

He'd go and talk to Seamus in the morning. He'd reassure him that there was nothing between him and the girl and that he was leaving for the north and to thank him for his many kindnesses.

John closed the door and read the telegram again, feeling a knot in his chest as he did. He should have never let Teddy go north by himself. He reached for the bottle of tequila.

The boy, Chico, had encamped himself outside the priest's window after a long day of labor. He'd purchased some warm tortillas and a bowl of frijoles for his supper and had eaten them with relish and haste. He often liked to eat his supper outside the priest's window whenever the priest did not invite him to supper and listen to the man some said was his father singing there in the evenings. But lately the priest had forgone his singing and had taken to drinking mescal and cursing God.

It was because of the woman that the priest drank and cursed. Because she often went lately to visit the other gringo. At first the priest didn't seem to mind, and often he invited the gringo to supper with him there in his hacienda and the three of them—the priest, the gringo and the woman would eat together. But lately the priest ate alone and drank alone and cursed the woman when she wasn't there and cursed himself and God.

So the boy felt badly for him, felt the priest's anger as well.

And so it was this particular night.

The woman had come in late and the priest had asked her if she'd gone to visit John Sears.

"You have, haven't you?" Chico heard the priest say.

Of course the woman was a mute and couldn't answer except by signaling with her hands or by writing it down.

Chico peered over the windowsill, saw the two of them there across the table from each other. The priest's face was flushed red and his movements uncertain. There on the table was an olla and a glass half full of the greasy brown liquor, some of it spilled on the table in a wet puddle.

The woman held her hands, palms outward, as if to ward off the priest's accusations. She shook her head no, the rope of her hair swaying.

The priest berated her and Chico could tell that he was drunk by the way he slurred his words and staggered.

"Oh, oh!" the priest said, then slumped into a chair and put his face into his hands. The woman tried to comfort him by placing her hands on his shoulders but he swept them aside.

"Betrayal," the priest said. "You've betrayed me and I've betrayed myself . . ."

The woman began crying, her sounds muffled but the tears wet on her cheeks, as wet as the stain of mescal on the table. She stood opposite the priest and cried.

The boy felt the betrayal and he decided in an instant what to do about it.

John had begun drinking as soon as the woman left. He had a hard ride tomorrow and probably harder still what lay ahead of him, and he'd need all his wits about him once he began the journey to either free his friend or kill the marshal, Hoodoo Brown. But tonight he would drink and try and free himself from his desire for the woman and every other bad thing he felt in his life.

And by the time the boy knocked on his door, John Sears was about as drunk as he'd ever been.

He lay on the bed listening to the knocking. He thought it was her, Selena: that she'd returned to plead with him to take her in.

"Go away," he said, reaching for the bottle of tequila he'd bought that very morning only to find that it was now empty.

*Knock, knock.*

He tried ignoring it.

*Knock, knock.*

"Oh, goddamn," he muttered and rose unsteadily from the bed and fumbled his way through the darkness to the door.

"Who is it . . . ?"

The boy was standing there with the pistol already in his hands.

John looked at it, looked into the boy's eyes— this same boy he'd seen almost every day, the one he knew as an orphan, the one who reminded him of himself when he was a boy, the one he'd taught to shoot the gun he was now holding.

The explosion carried John back into the room.

He could smell cordite but could not feel his arms or legs.

The sound of the gun still echoed in his brain.

He heard footsteps running.

He lay there thinking, so this is the way it ends.

He closed his eyes and thought, *Death, be quick, don't let me linger.*

The priest came.

He knelt beside John and took his head in his hands.

"He thought he was doing me a favor," the priest said. "I don't know how to excuse it . . ."

John could smell liquor on the priest's breath but it didn't matter. Those lucid eyes that looked into his were of some comfort and if there truly was a Jesus, John imagined he had eyes like those of the priest.

"Don't move me," John said.

John could see the faces of many of the villagers crowded in the doorway.

His breathing was becoming more difficult; he wasn't sure how much time had passed since he had been shot. He had passed out and then awakened again to find the priest kneeling next to him.

John turned his head and saw the woman there by the door, her face stained with tears.

"There was never anything to it," he said, his voice raspy. "Me and her . . ."

"It doesn't matter," the priest said.

"To me it does. I just want you to know I'd never . . ."

"Do you want me to give you last rites?"

"I ain't Catholic . . ."

"It doesn't matter."

"It can't hurt any if you did . . ."

The priest spoke words over him, rubbed the sign of the cross on his brow with his thumb. Some of what the priest said John heard, some of it he didn't, as he faded in and out of consciousness. It was like a bad dream he couldn't quite wake from, couldn't quite fall into completely.

"Is there someone you want me to contact?" the priest said. "Your friend, Teddy?"

"Tell him . . . tell him . . ."

The priest could see John's lips moving but could no longer hear what he was saying.

John's thumbless hand opened and closed.

In the dream, the long, forever dream that John was entering, he could see snow-capped mountains and a herd of wild mustangs racing across a ledge of land that was deep green with summer grasses. And between the horses and the mountains, he could see a large blue lake that looked like glass with the sun sparkling in it.

He reached out to touch the places he saw, to stroke the manes of the horses. Then he saw the woman coming toward him—the one he'd loved so desperately in Las Vegas and had killed. She had her arms outstretched, calling to him, *Come John . . .*

He looked back over his shoulder and he didn't like what he saw as much as what lay ahead of him and so he didn't turn back but kept walking toward the woman, the mountains, the wild horses, the blue lake.

"That's it," the priest said. "It is finished, he is no more." He closed John's eyes, knowing they had seen things that only the dead have seen in those last moments of their living.

The villagers crossed themselves and slunk away into the night, all except for a few women who said that they would wash the body and prepare the gringo for burial.

Selena had written something on a piece of paper that she handed to the priest:

*What about Chico?*

The priest shook his head. "I will find him," he said.

Selena made a motion with her hands.

"He did what he thought was the right thing to do, to protect us," the priest said. "Now we must protect him."

The woman made a sign with her hands that she was sorry.

The priest said, "I should be asking forgiveness from you," and took her and held her, knowing that some of the tears she wept were for the gringo and some for the boy and some for their love that had gone astray.

And all night the priest prayed for forgiveness

and when morning fell again on the village he removed the crucifix he wore and placed it beside his bible, then woke the woman and said, "It's time to go," then went and woke the boy and told him the same thing.

## Chapter 30

———◆———

Bat was crossing the street to reach the Dodge House when he heard gunshots, then glass shattering. He looked up and saw two men falling from the sky.

Teddy had delivered Mae to her boarding house.

"You will promise to let me know what your feelings are before you leave Dodge?" she said.

"Yes," he said.

He could tell that she wanted him to kiss her good night, and he *wanted* to kiss her good night but did not. He waited until she entered the house then drove the cab down to the livery and turned it in and walked back to his hotel.

The desk clerk stopped him and handed him a telegram.

"It arrived for you this afternoon," the clerk said.

Teddy put it in his pocket. He felt weary and only wanted a quiet room and a bed.

He climbed the stairs feeling the weight of the world on his shoulders.

Once inside the room, he struck a match to the lamp's wick and adjusted the flame to low. Then he turned and saw the man there in front of the window holding the pistol.

"Yeah, you're him," the man said.

"I'm who, and what the hell are you doing here?"

"You're the feller named Blue and I'm here to kill you."

"Kill me why?"

"Cause I'm getting paid to, that simple enough for you? You want, you can close your eyes. It wouldn't be no shame in it if you was to, lots of men have."

"Who's paying you to kill me?"

The man grunted. "I guess it don't matter you was to know it's Bone Butcher. He's mighty pissed you shot his toes off. You gone close your eyes or you want to see it coming?"

Teddy knew there was no way he could pull the Lightning and fire before the man shot him, but he wasn't about to go down without fighting.

His hand snaked inside his coat.

The man said, "Fine, you son of a bitch," and pulled the trigger, but nothing happened. They both knew the hammer fell on a dud and Teddy knew he had less than a split second to make his move.

He charged the man and knocked his arm aside just as he pulled the trigger a second time. The pistol discharged and the bullet slammed through the floor, striking the desk clerk in the wrist.

Teddy had the man's shooting hand in a death grip, but before he could wrest the gun from him, the man fired again. This time, the bullet ripped through Teddy's coat.

With a lunge, he and the man crashed through the window and for a full moment they were falling free. Then they slammed against the porch overhang and lost their grip on one another, Teddy falling away from the man before hitting the ground.

He realized he still had the man's gun he'd wrested free, but it felt of little consequence as he struggled to regain his breath. The man lay several feet away.

Bat ran up, bent over Teddy and turned him over, then saw who one of the men was that'd fallen from the sky. "Blue!"

Teddy couldn't quite get the warning words out as he saw the other man rise to his knees behind Bat and draw a second revolver from his boot, cock and aim it. Teddy fired from where he lay, through Bat's spraddled legs, and saw the bullet knock the man backwards.

Bat stood stunned for a pure instant, not realizing exactly what was going on, then turned slightly, enough to see the dead gunman.

"What the hell—"

"Bone Butcher sent him," Teddy gasped.

Bat went nearer and examined the man's face.

"It's the son of a bitch who shot Hoodoo Brown," Bat said. "Name's Two Bits Cline. And I'm guessing he's the one who shot Frenchy Le-Breck and the Rose too, her dead as him."

"Frenchy's dead?" Teddy said.

"As you can get," Bat said. "I found them just a while ago in Frenchy's place, was coming to warn you there might be another shooter."

Teddy thought, *At least Frenchy died with the woman he loved*, sad as that fact seemed.

Bat helped Teddy to his feet.

"What do you say we go finish this?" Teddy said.

"My sentiments exactly."

Bone was in his office, his bad foot resting still on the fancy pillow, a glass of top-shelf bourbon near his one hand, the little silver-plated pistol near his right. He heard footsteps approaching, figured it was Two Bits coming to collect his money. A smile creased his face.

*Come on and get your reward,* he thought, reaching for the pistol.

Only when the door opened and Bone fired, it wasn't Two Bits Cline he shot, but rather Bat's new derby, before Bat shot Bone through the forehead. It was a brief and unhappy surprise for Bone to see Bat Masterson and that feller who'd shot off his toes. And unhappier still to see Bat's pistol spit fire.

It was a clean accurate shot without compare.

Bat retrieved his derby, examined the hole in it.

"Cost me five dollars," he said.

Teddy saw the open safe, the stacks of money in it.

"I reckon the state wouldn't mind if Bone was to reimburse you for the hat."

"I reckon not."

"I think it's over," Teddy said.

"I think it's over too."

Teddy offered Bat his hand, and Bat shook it.

"I was all wrong about you," Bat said. "You're a damn good man and I'm damn glad you came to Dodge."

"I'll be leaving in the morning."

"You taking the flier?"

"Yeah."

"I'll come down and see you off."

"No need."

"I'd like to anyway."

Teddy glanced at the late Bone Butcher, saw that one of the soles of his shoes had a hole worn through it, saw again the money there in the safe and wondered why a man with so much would let his shoes get worn down. Well, it wouldn't matter now why; some men were just strange in their behavior. Bone would see the woman he supposedly loved dead rather than happy and he'd rather wear shoes with holes in them than pay to have them fixed. Such were the men that came to Dodge, Teddy reasoned. But then too, there were the Mastersons and Dog Kelly—men who cared to tame a wild town and make it better for everyone.

"See you around," Teddy said and walked out into the hard black night.

He started back to his hotel, then changed his mind and went to the boarding house where Mae stayed.

He asked the woman running the place for her room and the woman bid him wait in the parlor while she fetched Mae, citing the fact it was unseemly for a female boarder to have male visitors after dark alone in their rooms.

Teddy waited and in a few minutes Mae appeared.

She seemed surprised to see him, but relieved too.

"What is it?" she said.

"Something happened tonight," he said. "It made me think."

She waited for him to say what it was.

"I've come to realize how quickly our lives can be changed by a single act, something we don't expect to happen. I think that's how it was for you when Horace was killed, and I understand now that you had no hand in his death; it was just something that happened. And I can't blame you for the actions of your brother. I've come to care a great deal about you, Mae. I don't want us to part feeling badly toward each other. But more importantly, I don't want you to think I hold any animosity toward you. In fact, the truth of how I feel is just the opposite."

She came closer to him.

"I have to go away and take care of some things," he said. "I'll leave you my address in Chicago and if you leave Dodge before you hear from me, contact me there and I'll find you."

"Does this mean you think there is a real chance for us, Teddy?"

"I think there could be."

Her eyes welled with tears.

"I love you," she said.

"And I you."

"Kiss me before you go?"

He felt a sweet sadness for her as he kissed her and he felt the same sweet sadness the next day as he waited for the flier to pull into the station.

Bat was there and so was Ed, leaning on a pair of crutches, and so was Dog Kelly, looking tired with red eyes.

"Hell of a job, young man," Dog said patting him on the shoulder. "I'll send along word to your boss what grand work you performed here."

"No need," Teddy said. "Generally if any of his operatives come back alive, George is pleased."

"You ever want to leave the Pinkertons and come west again," Ed said, "I could use me a good deputy."

"Same here," Bat said.

"You boys look to me like you got it all covered," Teddy said.

"Well, not quite all," Bat said.

Ed looked sheepish.

"How so?" Teddy said.

"That damn Dirty Dave Rudabaugh somehow managed to live and has escaped from the infirmary and we can't find him anyplace."

Dog leaned and spat and said, "Shit, I reckon he can't be killed or caught, he's got more lives than a cat."

"Oh, we'll catch him," Bat said. "Or somebody will."

They all laughed at the ludicrousness of the situation.

It was starting to snow.

"Winter looks like it's finally here to stay," Dog said.

Teddy shook their hands and boarded the train.

He fought the urge to go and find Mae and take her with him. He fought the urge to stay and maybe make a life for himself here in Dodge, the Bibulous Babylon of the plains.

And when the train at last pulled out and he waved his last good-bye and watched as the train's shadow rode over the endless prairies, he thought he could see in the great distance a man riding a horse. A man who looked like maybe he wasn't feeling so good but riding hellbent anyway—riding hard away from Dodge.

Then he remembered the telegram and pulled it from his pocket and saw that it was from Juarez.